"Is  asked
Winn

Nick gave her a wicked grin. "I thought you'd never ask."

Fiona wanted to go back to the hotel, take a cold shower, and crawl into bed—alone—but from the look on Nick's face, he had something else in mind.

The thought of sliding between the covers with Nick sent her pulse pounding. She was certain her cheeks were fire-hot just thinking about what this man could do to her body. She struggled to banish the thought and gathered her wits. "That's not what I meant. Besides, you can't leave—Winnie's counting on you."

Nick glanced toward Winnie and Walter, then smiled at Fiona. "They'll never miss us."

"If we leave together, they'll draw conclusions about us," she said, frowning.

Nick looked interested. "Oh, and what conclusion might that be?"

"The, uh, obvious," she said, hoping the answer would satisfy him.

"The obvious? You mean, that we're sneaking away to make mad, passionate love together?"

Nick teased a wisp of hair that blew across her cheek, and Fiona drew a quick breath at his touch. "Nick—"

"Maybe we shouldn't let a good conclusion go to waste. . . ."

WHAT ARE *LOVESWEPT* ROMANCES?

They are stories of true romance and touching emotion. We believe those two very important ingredients are constants in our highly sensual and very believable stories in the LOVESWEPT line. Our goal is to give you, the reader, stories of consistently high quality that may sometimes make you laugh, sometimes make you cry, but are always fresh and creative and contain many delightful surprises within their pages.

Most romance fans read an enormous number of books. Those they truly love, they keep. Others may be traded with friends and soon forgotten. We hope that each LOVESWEPT romance will be a treasure—a "keeper." We will always try to publish

LOVE STORIES YOU'LL NEVER FORGET
BY AUTHORS YOU'LL ALWAYS REMEMBER

The Editors

HERE COMES THE BRIDE

GAYLE KASPER

BANTAM BOOKS
NEW YORK · TORONTO · LONDON · SYDNEY · AUCKLAND

HERE COMES THE BRIDE
A Bantam Book / July 1995

LOVESWEPT *and the wave design are registered trademarks of Bantam Books, a division of Bantam Doubleday Dell Publishing Group, Inc. Registered in U.S. Patent and Trademark Office and elsewhere.*

All rights reserved.
Copyright © 1995 by Gayle Kasper.
Back cover art copyright © 1995 by George Tsui.
Floral border by Joyce Kitchell.
No part of this book may be reproduced or transmitted in any form or by any means, electronic or mechanical, including photocopying, recording, or by any information storage and retrieval system, without permission in writing from the publisher.
For information address: Bantam Books.

If you purchased this book without a cover you should be aware that this book is stolen property. It was reported as "unsold and destroyed" to the publisher and neither the author nor the publisher has received any payment for this "stripped book."

If you would be interested in receiving protective vinyl covers for your Loveswept books, please write to this address for information:

Loveswept
Bantam Books
P.O. Box 985
Hicksville, NY 11802

ISBN 0-553-44318-6

Published simultaneously in the United States and Canada

Bantam Books are published by Bantam Books, a division of Bantam Doubleday Dell Publishing Group, Inc. Its trademark, consisting of the words "Bantam Books" and the portrayal of a rooster, is Registered in U.S. Patent and Trademark Office and in other countries. Marca Registrada. Bantam Books, 1540 Broadway, New York, New York 10036.

PRINTED IN THE UNITED STATES OF AMERICA

OPM   0 9 8 7 6 5 4 3 2 1

To the Las Vegas girls—
Barb, Diane, Ethel, and Shannon

ONE

Fiona Ames sat on her suitcase in the middle of the baggage-claim area at Las Vegas's McCarran Airport, wilting in her white wool suit as she searched for her transportation.

And then she saw him.

For twenty minutes she'd scanned the crowd, wondering how she would recognize a man she'd never met. All she had was a vague general description—tall, dark, and handsome. But when it happened, when she saw the tan leather suitcase split open on the baggage carousel and disperse its contents, her quick speculation became absolute certainty.

Male underwear, skimpy, silk, and lurid, tumbled out along with a few tame shirts and a blow-dryer.

Fiona glanced away, hoping that when she returned her gaze, the owner of the bag wouldn't fit the description of the man she was supposed to meet.

He did—in spades.

She shouldn't have expected less, though, given how her day had begun.

She had to admire his aplomb—or was it brass?—the way he gathered up the sexy briefs, returning the smiles of feminine onlookers without missing a beat. Several of his admirers looked ready to offer him their hotel keys—and he looked ready to accept.

Maybe she was wrong. Maybe this wasn't the man she would be sharing a ride with from the airport. He could be here for any number of reasons, *logical* reasons—such as . . . an underwear convention. But when the man zipped his bag closed again and turned around, his blue-eyed gaze scouring the terminal, she knew he was searching for her.

Fiona's white wool suddenly grew warmer.

He was handsome, in that hard, lean, illicit sort of way that held women in thrall. His deep tan gave him a decadent look, as if he did nothing more ambitious all day than sip tall drinks poolside. The ends of his rich brown hair were sun-tipped and ruffled, curling carelessly over his shirt collar.

She noticed the well-fitting cut of his light-colored suit and caught herself wondering if he had a pair of those racy briefs on

Here Comes the Bride

beneath. Maybe in a wild island print, a palm tree swaying seductively over his—

Fiona checked the direction of that thought.

She wasn't in Nevada to think about what the man wore next to his . . . tan. She was there for her father's wedding, a wedding that would take place tomorrow—that was, unless she could find some way to put a stop to the ceremony before then.

But that was a problem she would deal with later—after she'd gotten to her hotel, and peeled off these hot clothes and her panty hose that had sprung a half-inch-wide run somewhere over Denver.

Still, she knew that unless she wanted to wilt outside waiting for a taxi, Mr. Sexy was her best bet for a ride. Fiona dragged in a deep, steadying breath and started toward him.

"Mr. Killian? Nick Killian?" she asked as she neared.

He raised one dark eyebrow and his speculative male gaze skimmed over her. "Miss Ames?"

His voice was low, self-assured, and seductive—like the man. It had a slow drawl to it, a sensually erotic quality that stirred Fiona to her nail beds. "I'm Fiona Ames."

That dangerous smile edged his lips. "I

hope I didn't keep you waiting," he said. "I had a small, uh, mishap with my luggage."

"I saw."

At that moment the baggage carousel made a full revolution, and rotating slowly toward them was a skimpy scrap of leopard print. Fiona considered ignoring the hot item and ushering him toward the door, but unfortunately he saw it too.

"Yours, I believe," she said.

He only grinned, a slow, sexy slash in his tanned face. Fiona was not about to let the silk go around again for all to see—at least as long as she was standing there beside him. She reached down and plucked it off the carousel.

He didn't even have the good grace to look embarrassed, only amused, and Fiona realized that she was the one caught holding the silky scrap. The smile on his face made her feel as if she had her hands on his body instead of just his rakish underwear.

"Here," she said. She shoved the silk undies at his midsection, then wished she hadn't. It was rock-hard beneath his pale blue shirt, just as she'd imagined it would be.

"Thanks." His naughty grin widened. "This is my favorite pair." The silk danced between them for what seemed like forever before he finally stuffed them into the pocket of his jacket. "Do you always blush like that?" he asked, tucking a finger beneath her chin.

Here Comes the Bride

Fiona wasn't in the habit of blushing, and she didn't know why she was now, except that this man seemed to provoke that response in her. Or maybe it was fondling his seductive underwear. Whatever had prompted the blush, she wasn't about to admit to it.

"It's the heat. I'll adjust," she snapped back. She reached for the strap on her suitcase and tugged the thing along as she headed for the nearest exit.

Nick hadn't been at all enthused about winning the silky briefs at that bachelor auction for charity his long-time friend and frat brother had coerced him into in New York. He'd been less enthused seeing the undies tumble out of his bag on the carousel. That was, until he watched the hot color rise up Fiona Ames's pretty neck.

Nick grinned as he picked up his bag and followed her. If he'd enjoyed the way the lady blushed, he enjoyed the sassy swing to her hips in that snug white skirt even more. Sexy, *very* sexy, he decreed.

He suspected she'd be stripping out of that white wool damned fast in this climate though, and for one unvirtuous moment he found himself wishing he could be there for the show. He stopped the momentum of that thought. Fiona Ames was hardly the kind of woman he was accustomed to. Too haughty for his tastes. Still, she had him intrigued.

Her flame-red hair was pulled into a knot at the back of her head, no doubt in deference to the heat, but wispy ends refused to be tamed and flew around her face in tight little coils. He wondered if that might be a clue to her personality as well—tightly coiled yet a part of her refusing to be tamed. The prospect of that combination stirred him, perhaps more than it should have.

This upcoming wedding might prove more interesting than he thought.

In his heart of hearts he doubted Walter Ames was any match for his aunt. Winnie claimed she'd fallen in love at first sight, but Nick didn't believe there was such a thing.

He didn't believe in love at all.

Maybe if he hadn't been out of town so much the last few months, consulting on those legal cases, he might have headed off this fiasco. Still, the wedding bells hadn't chimed yet.

They'd reached the curb. He motioned to the waiting limousine driver, and when the limo pulled up, he escorted his pretty passenger inside.

"I hope dropping me at my hotel doesn't inconvenience you," she said, sliding into her seat.

The hem of her skirt skimmed up a delicious inch or two. And he noticed that she had a run in her nylons. He followed the streak up her leg until it disappeared beneath the white fabric. Quickly he chastised his mind's eye, which seemed hell-bent on tracing it farther up her silky thigh. Her blush had faded, at least for the moment. But he'd like very much to see it again.

"Winnie asked me to see you safely to your hotel and to make sure you were comfortable. It was fortunate we were arriving at the same time. Did you have a good trip out?"

"Yes, fine," she returned. She didn't add that she'd spent nearly every moment of her air time trying to decide what to do about her father and his sudden wedding plans. Fiona hadn't even known there was a woman in his life until this morning when he'd phoned, asking her to fly out for the ceremony.

Since Nick's aunt was the blushing bride-to-be, she didn't want to bring up the subject with him. Winnie was probably a very nice lady—Fiona wasn't saying that she wasn't—she just didn't want to see her father make a mistake that might well cost him his happiness. She loved him too much to let that happen.

Walter Ames hadn't been able to come to the airport to meet her himself because he was busy having his tux fitted for the ceremony, thus abandoning Fiona to the man seated beside her, a man whose good looks and intense masculinity rattled her senses.

She pressed a hand to her temple, thinking of the fast trip she'd made across the country. If it wasn't for her father and his hasty wedding she would be home right now, polishing antiques for her shop and planning an evening at the symphony with friends.

Nick Killian—and his sexy briefs—were about as far removed from a night at the symphony as she could imagine.

Fiona leaned back in her seat and swung one leg over the other, trying hard to ignore his presence.

She supposed she could use the few days off this trip would bring. She'd been working hard, too hard. But her shop was important to her. She'd struggled to turn it into the business she'd envisioned, a shop where people could come and feel welcome, sip a cup of tea while they browsed, and hopefully buy an heirloom-quality antique.

She could count on Elaine to keep an eye on things while she was away. Elaine was her good friend, who owned the photography studio next to Fiona's small shop in the little row of businesses a few blocks off the Common. She'd promised to take in the mail and explain to Fiona's loyal customers that she'd been called away on a family matter.

Fiona hadn't realized the *family* would include the man who had her on the edge of her limo seat, feeling as gawky as a teenager on a first date. At twenty-nine she was well past her awkward teen years, but she supposed when it came to men like Nick Killian, she was still a babe-in-the-woods.

After suffering through one failed engagement she'd learned to be more cautious of relationships. Adam Parker had hurt her, hurt her *badly*. And she didn't intend to become vulnerable again. Perhaps it was advice she should pass along to her father. What did he really know about Winnie? She could be someone who would break his heart.

And that Fiona couldn't bear.

Perhaps heartbreaking ran in the family. She'd bet her airline ticket home that Nick Killian could break a few hearts. He had that all-too-persuasive, love-'em-and-leave-'em air about him—along with killer-wide shoulders and a smile that could promise a woman the world.

"Is it always this hot out here?" she asked, feeling a heat she suspected wasn't entirely attributable to the desert.

"This isn't Boston, if that's what you mean. But I'll ask the driver to adjust the air," Nick offered.

"Thanks." Fiona doubted it would help all that much. Nick was sitting so close that his muscled thigh was pressed up against her. And from there it was only a small leap of her imagination to his provocative underwear.

She tried to tell herself she didn't care if they were polka-dot boxers, but she knew that wasn't quite true.

Before meeting him, she had never thought about a man's . . . personables. She fanned herself with a travel brochure she'd picked up while she was waiting at the baggage claim, then stared out through the tinted windows, studying the buildings in the distance that seemed to rise right up off the desert floor, a hazy mirage in front of her.

"I hope you brought something cooler to wear tonight," Nick said beside her. "If not, there are a couple of shops in your hotel."

"Tonight?" Fiona stopped fanning herself and turned to him, one eyebrow raised. "What's tonight?"

"Didn't your father tell you?"

It seemed her father hadn't been telling her much of anything lately. "Tell me what?"

"We're invited to Winnie's for dinner. She thought it would be nice if we all sort of . . . got acquainted."

Fiona's eyes widened. A get-acquainted dinner—of course that would be in the plans. They were, after all, about to become . . . family. Still, she'd hoped to see her father alone tonight.

She had more than a few questions to ask him.

"I—I'm not sure I can make it this evening," she stammered.

Nick smiled. "We don't have a choice in the matter. Winnie's expecting us. Eight o'clock sharp."

A command performance. Fiona sank back in her seat, certain there was no way out of the invitation. She wasn't ready to meet Winnie yet. *Or* spend more time with the woman's distracting nephew.

The limo eased through the bumper-to-bumper traffic on the Strip. Nick pointed out the major casinos glittering under the hot desert sun. Fiona tried to ignore the brush of his thigh against hers, his nearness, his provocative male scent that was having such a disturbing effect on her.

"Ah, we're here," he said when they'd finally turned into the hotel's sweeping drive.

"Let's get you checked in," Nick said when the driver held the limo door open for them.

"I think I can manage that by myself." She forced a polite smile and extended her hand. "Thank you for the lift."

He took her hand, his touch drawing her to him as intimately as an embrace. She could feel the sensual heat of him, the threat of what the man had to offer. It had to do with sin and seduction and hot, steamy nights.

A dangerous fantasy, she knew. But she

was a woman—and Nick Killian had a way of making her vibrantly aware of that fact.

Disengaging her hand from his, she slid out of the limo and headed for the revolving hotel door, leaving Nick behind and the driver to retrieve her luggage.

Nick watched her go. An enigmatic smile crept to his lips. He hadn't been looking forward to this evening at Auntie's—that was, until now.

Fiona Ames heated his blood in a way that no woman had in a long time—maybe ever. He recognized a certain danger in that, but Nick had never been afraid of getting too close to the flame.

After a shower and a much-needed and all-too-short nap, Fiona searched through her wardrobe for the coolest dress she'd brought with her. She settled on a sleeveless white linen and slipped it on. The dress had a deep V-neck that she'd never noticed dipped quite so low. She ran a finger over the front and caught herself wondering what Nick Killian would think of it.

What did she care what he thought? The man had a way of making her swelter—and at least this dress would be cool. She added a pair of round gold earrings, dashed on a touch of geranium-pink lipstick that the saleslady said was perfect for redheads, and studied the effect in the mirror.

Would Nick think her mouth looked kissable?

Forget it, she told herself. You don't want to know.

She smoothed down a pleat in the skirt, then grabbed her purse and headed for the front entrance to meet her father. She'd talked to him on the phone shortly after she'd checked in, but their discussion had been as unfruitful as the one this morning. She needed to get him alone and talk face-to-face. If only they didn't have this evening at Winnie's.

She made her way through the crowded lobby and reached the hotel's front entrance just as Walter Ames wheeled his ancient Buick into the circular drive. Some things never change, she thought, and smiled at the sensible sedan that was her father's pride and joy.

He'd come to the desert a few months earlier, deciding he could no longer take the New England winters. She'd known he was lonely. Ever since her mother had died three years before, he'd been at loose ends. But his abrupt move to Las Vegas had been a surprise.

As much of a surprise as his wedding tomorrow.

She opened the door and slid in beside him.

"There's my girl," he said, giving Fiona a warm hug.

Despite her irritation with him she was genuinely glad to see him. She inhaled his familiar scent. "Oh, Dad, I've missed you."

"And it took my wedding to get you out here."

His wedding. They needed to talk about that, but Fiona decided it could wait. She wanted to assure herself he was all right. Really all right.

"How have you been, Dad?" she asked. She studied the face of the man who'd been there for her so many times in her life. "Getting too much sun, I see." She reached over and rubbed his peeling nose.

"Maybe a little," he said. "But the sun is good for me. In fact, I haven't felt this great in years."

"Well, I'm glad to hear that."

He wheeled the big old Buick out of the hotel drive and headed down the congested Strip. Gaudy lights winked and blinked in neon fury, making Fiona long for home, the charm of Boston. She missed her shop, filled to overflowing with antiques, and her apartment over it, small, comfortable, and homey.

She'd been experiencing a kind of culture shock ever since she'd arrived in Las Vegas—and she wasn't sure she could survive it.

"You're going to love Winnie, Fiona. I can

hardly wait for you to meet her," her father said, glancing over at her. A beatific, if not a bit foolish, smile covered his face.

He was a man in love, a development that worried Fiona. She drew in a breath. "Dad, about this wedding—"

"Now, don't you worry about the wedding plans, Fiona. They're all taken care of. There's not a thing for you to do but show up and wish your father happiness."

"That wasn't what I meant, Dad. Your happiness is first and foremost in my mind, believe me . . ." This wasn't going to be an easy discussion, but she had to try to make him see reason. Now might be the only chance she had to convince him to wait, to think things through, to look before he leaped into this marriage thing.

"Then what, Fiona?" A furrow formed between his sandy-gray brows. "I thought you'd be happy for me."

Fiona sighed and studied a flashing block-long marquee that brightened the night as if it were midday. He'd phoned out of the blue, springing this wedding on her, wanting her to be happy about it. But how could she be happy about a romance that had seemingly blossomed overnight?

She thought of her parents' marriage. It had lasted thirty years, a hearts-and-flowers, old-fashioned kind of marriage few people in life ever achieved—the kind Fiona wanted for herself one day. But a love like that took time to develop and to grow.

"I *am* happy for you, Dad," she said, seriously trying to mean it.

"Well, you could've fooled me." He turned and headed west, toward a bank of mountains in the distance, away from the gaudy bright lights of the Strip.

Fiona tried again. "Dad, what do you know about Winnie? Does she have family?" she asked. He had told her very little about his intended on the phone. All Fiona knew was her name and that she had a nephew who wore racy underwear.

He braked at a stoplight and glanced over at her. "Yes, she has a family. A very loving family . . ."

As opposed to his nonunderstanding daughter, Fiona read into that statement.

"Winnie lost her husband some years ago," he said, pulling through the light and continuing west. "She's alone. Like me."

Fiona felt a stab of pain that her father thought of himself as being alone. He had her, after all. And he had memories of her mother. Wonderful memories of the life they'd shared together. Ashamed, she wondered for the first time if that was really enough to sustain him. Or did he need more? Did he need someone like Winnie?

"What about children? Does Winnie have children?"

"She has a daughter, about your age. She won't be able to come to the wedding, though. She's off working in India or Istanbul or . . . someplace. And then there's her nephew Nick, of course."

Nick. As if Fiona could have forgotten.

Wickedly handsome, incredibly sexy Nick.

"Dad, I know you already have your plans made, but don't you think you should wait, think this thing through, be sure you . . . ? Be sure you're both ready?" she finished. She couldn't bring herself to say "love each other." After all, there hadn't been enough time for that. "What's the rush anyway?"

"Rush? Fiona, when you get to be my age, you don't know how many years you have left. Rush becomes a priority."

Fiona gave her father a long, considering look. His once-auburn hair had turned a sandy gray, but he had a full head of it. His hazel eyes were bright, his mind sharp. He was sixty-five, hardly ancient; he didn't have to snatch at life as if he were about to draw his last breath.

He was a nice-looking man with a straight, proud spine and square, wide shoulders and a lady-killer smile. She hadn't realized it until now, but she could see how he could have any number of women chasing him.

"I hope you'll be nice tonight, Fiona. This is important to me."

Fiona rubbed her throbbing temples. "I know, Dad."

The old Buick swept into a neighborhood of lush green lawns, an oasis in the middle of the desert, kept verdant by spouting water sprinklers.

Winnie's house was sprawling and white and coolly inviting, yet Fiona dreaded entering it. She was just thinking she'd sooner walk barefoot across the desert than go through with this evening, when a woman swooped down on them in a purple cloud of swirling skirts. A dozen silver Indian bracelets clanked on her right arm.

"So this is your daughter," Winnie said. "She's lovely, Walter. It's nice to meet you, Fiona. How was your flight out?"

She chatted with Fiona on their way to the front door, barely giving her time to answer one question before launching into another. Fiona had to smile at this small tornado of a woman who'd obviously swept her father off his feet. He probably never knew what hit him.

"Why didn't you tell me how enchanting your daughter is, Walter?" Winnie scolded, then reached up and gave him a peck on the cheek.

Her father blushed a bright shade. He

wasn't a man who was big on outward displays of affection, but Winnie apparently was. Fiona knew it was a fact that opposites attract, but how did they fare over the long haul?

Winnie didn't allow her time to ponder this further, but led her guests across the large entry hall, her azalea-pink, high-heeled sandals tapping a staccato beat on the cool terrazzo tiles.

The home was as flamboyant as its owner. Brilliant bursts of color filled every room, not the muted desert hues Fiona would have expected, but exotic blues and sunny yellows and vivid purples that somehow all went together.

"We're having dinner beside the pool tonight," Winnie said, leading the way. "I hope you like rutabaga-and-lamb kabobs, Fiona. I fixed them especially for your father because he just loves them."

Fiona's eyes widened in surprise. Her father never ate lamb and he would have looked askance at a rutabaga if her mother had ever set one in front of him.

"That's Dad's favorite, all right," she said, sending a questioning glance in his direction.

"Be nice, Fiona," her father reminded in a whisper close to her ear. When she flared an eyebrow impudently, he added a stern frown to his admonition.

"Nicholas is here already," Winnie went on. "It's so lovely to have our two families together. I only wish Camille could be here with us, but she's away, working in the wilds of India."

Fiona wouldn't mind being in the wilds of India herself at the moment. She followed Winnie toward the pool area, where she glimpsed Nick tending the lamb kabobs on the grill. He had a tall drink in one hand, a long fork in the other, and he looked as decadently handsome as he had earlier that day.

"You already know Nicholas, I believe," Winnie said with a wave at her provocative nephew.

"We've met, Auntie," Nick said. He put down the fork and came toward Fiona, that slow, lazy smile of his teasing at his lips. His tan appeared even darker under the twinkling patio lights. He'd changed into a black polo shirt and cream-colored slacks that hugged his well-muscled thighs and did strange things to Fiona's equilibrium. She tried to tell herself it was just the desert heat. In a few days she'd adjust.

Nick politely exchanged greetings with Fiona's father, then glanced back at her, his gaze taking full measure. She felt its thoroughness all the way to her toes.

"Nicholas, why don't you fix Fiona a drink?" Winnie suggested. "And, Walter, you can help me set out the plates and silverware on the table."

She led him away, leaving Fiona alone with Nick.

"What can I get for you?" he asked with a wave of his hand toward a small bar set up at one end of the pool.

"Scotch," she said, never having tasted the stuff before, but sensing that tonight she would need it.

"Scotch it is," he said, but not before raising one dark eyebrow at her choice of liquor. He turned and started for the bar.

The man was good-looking, she couldn't deny that. And all male, right down to his sexy silk—

He turned around with her drink in his hand and caught where her gaze lingered. That slow smile of his slid onto his lips. He walked over to her and leaned close, his voice a low whisper next to her ear.

"They're tiger stripes," he drawled.

TWO

"Pardon me?"

"My underwear. They're tiger stripes. I thought you might be . . . wondering." Nick saw that blush of hers again. He gave a slow grin. He shouldn't take such delight in getting a rise out of her, but he couldn't help himself. That shade of pink looked provocative on her.

"Sorry to disappoint you, but I don't care if they're iridescent blue spangles," she returned haughtily, then snatched the drink from his hand and took a hard swallow.

"Oh? My mistake." He gave an easy shrug but continued to study her carefully. She was still wearing white, but not wool this time. His gaze trailed over the length of her and he realized he liked what he saw.

Fiona could feel the heat of Nick's gaze. She glanced across the patio to where her father was helping Winnie anchor the napkins under the plates before the things could become airborne in the light evening breeze, wishing she could put some distance between Nick and herself.

Nick turned to glance at the pair as well. "I advised Auntie to have Walter sign a prenuptial agreement I took the liberty of drawing up," he said.

That got Fiona's attention. She spun around, her flashing green eyes meeting the cool blue of his. "You did *what*?"

"I advised Auntie—"

"I heard you the first time," she snapped in irritation. "What I want to know is, whatever for?"

"To protect her, of course."

"Protect her? From what? From whom?"

"From your father. You can't be too careful, especially about things like money. Auntie has a lot of it, and I'd be remiss if I didn't look after her best interests."

Fiona dragged in a deep breath and set her drink down with a brisk thunk. "Let me get this straight," she said, glowering up at the man in front of her. "You think my father is . . . is—?"

"A womanizer," Nick finished.

Walter Ames wouldn't take a dime of someone else's money—especially a woman's. He was a proud man, a man with old-

Here Comes the Bride

fashioned values. If he wanted to marry Winnie, it certainly wasn't because of her money.

She couldn't believe she was hearing this. "Now wait just one minute," she said, planting her hands on her hips. "My father is not, and never has been, a . . . a . . ." She couldn't even say the word, and she was angry at Nick for thinking it. "Just what gives you the right to judge him?"

He dragged a hand over the back of his neck. "Look, I'm a lawyer. And Auntie's legal counsel. I'm sorry if you're offended by this but—"

"Offended? Is that what you think I am?"

Nick smiled. No, she was more like an avenging angel, he thought. Hot and volatile and gorgeous. Tonight she'd worn that thick, curly mane of red hair down. It teased at her creamy neck and skimmed the tops of her shoulders. Shoulders that were squared at the moment to do battle. Her eyes were wide and green and flashing fury in defense of her father.

He loved that stance, her beautiful chin raised a fractious notch, her pink-manicured hands on the rounded curve of her hips, one gold-sandaled toe tapping in front of him. It was enough to unnerve a lesser man.

Hell, it was enough to unnerve him.

She should wear white all the time, he thought. It made her skin look flawless, as pearly as a ten-dollar poker chip. He'd been trying to keep his gaze off that delectable neckline that showed the tiniest hint of cleavage, but it was a losing battle.

"You're right, *offended* is too mild a word," he said. "However, look at this from my point of view. What do I really know about Walter Ames?" Besides the fact that he has one tempting daughter, he thought quietly. "Nothing. He could be a gigolo, a con man, a . . ." He was making this worse, had her fur really flying now. He eased off. "Look, your father could very well be a nice man, good, decent. But the truth is, this wedding popped up too damn fast."

"Exactly," she chimed in. "And what do I know about your aunt Winnie? Zippo."

She was turning the tables. Neatly. Nick hid a grin. He liked that. "Hold that thought," he said, not wanting to end the conversation, not wanting to miss the fire in those beautiful eyes. "I think the kabobs need turning."

He shagged across the patio. They did, he realized, and he deftly flipped them over.

"Where were we?" he asked, when he turned around to find her behind him. "Need a refill on your drink?"

Fiona shook her head. She was certain she'd had enough scotch for one evening. In fact, she'd had enough of the evening.

Here Comes the Bride

If only she could grab her father by the shirt collar and drag him away. Away from this family who believed he was some kind of gold digger.

"You were saying something about Aunt Winnie, I believe." He took a swallow of his drink, eyeing her over the rim.

Fiona dragged in a breath. She didn't want to say anything derogatory about the woman. She'd just been trying to make a point. "Not about your aunt, but about the wedding plans. You're right. This has all happened too quickly. I think they need to wait, perhaps until they know each other better. They might find they're not at all suited to one another." Men could be very susceptible to whirlwind romances. Easily led down a primrose path before they knew what had hit them.

She glanced up at Nick. She could not in her wildest imagination see *him* being led down any primrose path. No matter how enticing the woman.

He was a man who knew his way around in this world. And it hadn't taken any suitcase of lady-killer briefs to tell her that. Everything about him bespoke maleness. Powerful maleness. She just wished that fact didn't send little shivers racing over her skin.

She glanced up as Nick let out a low chuckle. "Just what are we arguing about here?" he asked. "You don't approve of this wedding any more than I do." He studied her long and hard as if enjoying the idea of their being on the same side. "If we're smart we'd put our heads together and work out some way to foil tomorrow's little ceremony."

Fiona just wanted the pair to think about what they were doing. Marriage was a major step, not one to be taken lightly. "Foil it? Short of kidnapping the two of them, how do you expect to do that?"

She doubted very much that Nick could come up with an effective plan on such short notice. Besides, pooling brain power with this man was a little more togetherness than she thought wise. It made her nervous. She didn't like having to spend more time in his company than was absolutely necessary.

"Unless we want to watch them march down that aisle tomorrow, we're going to have to come up with something," he continued.

Fiona sighed. She knew it wasn't their place to interfere, but she *was* afraid her father was making a terrible mistake.

She massaged her tense neck. "Okay," she said. "It may already be too late to do anything, but we'll give it a try."

Dinner was strained at best. Walter and Winnie held hands and smiled at each other besottedly all through the meal, while Nick and Fiona frowned. The couple didn't seem to notice. Or that the conversation flagged.

The possibility that she and Nick sway this impetuous twosome looked bleak indeed.

When dinner was finished, Nick scraped back his chair. "It looks like you two want to be alone. Why don't I drop Fiona at her hotel, maybe even show her some of the town's nightlife along the way?"

"Oh, that's nice of you, dear," Winnie exclaimed. "I did want Walter to stay and help me decide about the placement of the flowers in the gazebo for the ceremony."

Fiona's mouth gaped open. Before she could object, Nick assisted her up from her seat and whispered in her ear, "Trust me."

Trust him? The man wanted to take her away from her father when time was a scarce commodity. She wasn't about to trust him.

"What do you think you're doing?" she snapped a few minutes later as they cleared the table. Fiona dogged his heels, carrying a stack of dishes inside. "I don't want to see this town's nightlife and I don't want to go back to my hotel."

"We need a plan if we're going to stall the wedding. And we can't very well have a strategy session right here under their noses, now, can we?"

They'd reached the kitchen. Fiona slid the dirty plates onto a peacock-blue tile countertop and faced him squarely. "A strategy session? What's wrong with setting them down and having a little heart-to-heart talk?"

Nick rinsed a plate and dropped it into the dishwasher. "Wouldn't work. We'd come off sounding like irate parents lecturing a pair of willful teenagers. We're going to have to come up with something better."

"Like what?"

"Like I don't know yet. That's why we need to talk."

Fiona handed him another plate. "Why is it you're against this wedding?" she asked, gazing up at him. "Besides the ridiculous notion that you think my father chases women for their money?"

Maybe he shouldn't have said that. It had been a jaded thought, but after he'd seen Walter with Fiona, his mind had taken a right turn. The guy'd been a husband, a father, and though that didn't eliminate all men from the louse category, it did cast Walter in a more favorable light.

At least he would give him the benefit of the doubt for the time being.

"Statistics," he said dryly. "We live in the divorce capital of the country, the place where those made-in-heaven romances come to die."

She raised an eyebrow. "And that's what you think will happen to Walter and Winnie?"

"That's the odds, like 'em or not."

"And when it does, you believe my father will want a chunk of your aunt's money?"

He'd seen that—and worse—in his practice. What two people could do to each other in the name of love had ceased to surprise him a long time ago. He'd been an idealistic young lawyer once, had taken on no more than the usual number of divorce cases, but when the word got around that he always won his clients a sizable settlement, his caseload skyrocketed. He was the new young gun in town and soon he was trying celeb cases, not just for the impetuous of Hollywood, but for rich and powerful clients as well. The better he became at what he did, the less he liked it.

Sooner or later they all came, looking for the easy out, the painless divorce. Lately he'd been called to consult on some of the more difficult cases around the country.

That's where he'd been the past week—and what he'd seen hadn't exactly endeared the institution of marriage to him.

Fiona wondered how Nick had gotten so cynical in his thirty-some years. "Tell me," she said. "Did Winnie get my father to sign that prenuptial agreement?"

If she had, that should tell her father something about the woman he was about to marry.

Nick dropped in the last dish, then snapped the dishwasher closed and cranked the dial to WASH before he answered. "No, Auntie refused even to consider it. She said she and Walter didn't need any silly piece of paper like that, they were in love."

Winnie went up a notch or two in Fiona's estimation. "Good for her."

"Good for . . . ? I thought you were as much against this wedding as I am."

Fiona put her hands on her hips. "I just believe that if two people are going to marry, they should first and foremost trust each other."

He studied her warily for a long moment. "It isn't going to happen—the wedding, that is. Come on, we'll say our good-byes to the happy couple and get out of here."

"Look, Nick, I don't know what kind of a plan we can come up with by tomorrow. Maybe I should just try to talk to my father and you talk to Winnie and—"

"And you think that will work?"

"It may."

"And if it doesn't?"

Fiona gave a long, shuddering sigh. "Then we—"

"Burn down the gazebo?" Nick supplied.

She frowned.

"Come on." He took her by the elbow. "We'll think of something."

As they passed the bright yellow wall

phone in the kitchen, it jangled. "I'll get that and be right out," Nick said.

Fiona trekked off through the cool interior of the family room. As she made her way around the breezy rattan furniture, she wondered how her father would ever be comfortable in this house. She tried to picture just where Winnie would park his battered old recliner with the worn seat cushion, the one Fiona knew he'd never part with.

She dragged a hand through the thick sweep of her hair. Of course, she hadn't believed he'd ever eat rutabaga and lamb either —and tonight he'd polished off Winnie's kabobs like he was a man starving.

With a frown she started toward the patio.

"There you are, Fiona," Winnie greeted her. "I need your advice about the flowers. Walter's no help at all. Where's Nicholas?"

"He's on the phone."

"Oh." Winnie glanced toward the house for a moment, then turned her attention back to the gazebo. And Fiona. "I thought we might place a basket of orange blossoms on either side of the minister and trail pink floribundas over the side latticework. What do you think? I need a woman's opinion."

Fiona would prefer not to give her opinion, but short of being rude, there was little else she could do but follow her soon-to-be stepmother across the green carpet of lawn.

She tossed her father a visual plea for help before she did so, but he only returned it with that silly smile he'd been wearing lately.

"Auntie," Nick called from the patio. "It's Camille on the phone."

"Camille?" Winnie squealed, and was off like a shot to take the overseas call.

Nick had brought a cordless phone outdoors and handed it to his aunt.

While Winnie chatted and motioned frantically for Walter to join her, Nick sauntered across the lawn to Fiona. "We're not going to be singing the 'Wedding Bell Blues' tomorrow after all," he said, draping an arm around her shoulders.

Even that simple touch set off a chain reaction of emotions in Fiona. Tempestuous, wild emotions. "What are you saying?"

"Camille has decided to come home for the wedding and she wants us to hold up everything until she gets here." He lifted Fiona's chin with the tip of one finger. "That buys us the time we need."

Fiona won fifty-three dollars playing the dollar slots at Caesar's, then promptly lost it all again. "Easy come, easy go, I guess," she said, turning to Nick.

A sexy smile rolled across his lips. "The secret of this town is to know when to quit."

"It looks like the time is now," she said in dismay as she dipped her hand into the metal tray of the machine that a few moments before had held the easily gotten loot, and came up empty.

"I was hoping you'd buy me a drink, but now it looks like I'll have to do the buying," he said.

"It looks that way." She laughed, realizing she was having a good time—despite her unfortunate initiation into the world of Vegas gambling.

"I know just the place." Nick led her through the packed casino and out into the warm Nevada night.

The stars overhead competed with the bright lights of the Strip, but lost. The breeze was sensuous and light as it blew a strand of her hair across her cheek. She brushed it aside as she waited beside Nick for his car to be brought around.

She was glad now that he'd insisted on showing her some of his town. Glad she'd accepted. There was a fire to it, a vibrancy, a spell that was easily cast over the unwary.

Nick possessed the same vibrancy, the same fire. And she suspected he was more than capable of casting a spell over her. That was, if she wasn't on her guard against it.

A shiver of vulnerability shuddered through her.

When his car arrived he eased her inside. She settled back into her seat as he got behind the wheel. Carefully he edged the silver Porsche past an elegant old Rolls with polished gilt trim, past several waiting limos lacing the drive, then out onto the Strip.

"Where are we going?" she asked, glancing over at him.

He was silhouetted against the night, the bright glitter of neon dancing through his hair, turning his blue eyes the colors of the rainbow. He drove with one hand on the wheel, the other on the gear shift. She recognized the strength and power in his grip, his long, lean fingers, the cords in his forearms, the bulge of his biceps.

Curiosity teased at her, making her wonder what those arms would feel like wound around her, those fingers tripping over her skin. Her blood heated at the thought. Nick Killian was strong and compelling—and the sexiest man she'd ever encountered.

"Away from the bright lights and the crowds, someplace where we can talk," he said.

Why did the sound of his words send tremors through her? The thought of being alone with him made her heart pound like a jackhammer gone mad.

It was true they'd left the lights behind. The desert loomed dark and mysterious around them, the mountains in the distance wary sentinels.

With the car's top down, the wind teased and toyed with her hair, flipping the ends around her face. She felt strangely reckless, she supposed because she'd been freed, at least temporarily, from worrying about her troublesome parent.

But feeling reckless and free around the dangerous man seated beside her might not be safe. Still, she couldn't help how she felt.

"This is a spot the locals consider their private domain. They refuse to give it up to the tourists," Nick said, slowing for a turn into the curving drive of a place called the Desert Club. "We're actually very possessive about it."

"Perhaps they won't let me in, considering I'm not a local."

"They'll let you in; you're with me."

She was that.

He opened the car door for her, then his hand found her elbow in a proprietary grasp as he led her toward the red-canopied entrance.

"We'll take a table outside, under the stars," he said to the owner as the man came to greet them—or to check that they weren't tourists come to ruin the sanctity of his establishment. "And bring us two of your specialties," Nick added.

The specialty turned out to be something

smooth and potent and dangerous, Fiona thought as the first sip raised her body temperature another notch.

"It's called Night Velvet," Nick said around a braver swallow than she chanced. "Too strong?"

It slid down like the velvet in its name and made her bones melt. Or maybe it was a combination of the stars peeping down on them on the small enclosed veranda and the man smiling across the table at her. His teeth were like rich, white pearls in the moonlight, even and perfect in his tanned face. They could nip a woman's skin and make her beg for more, she thought, letting her wanton imagination stray too far.

"It's fine," she said, then absently fingered a small bud vase on the table that held an orange desert flower. She didn't know if the flower had a fragrance to it or if it was the sweet night air around her mingled with the exciting scent of the man she was with.

She swallowed hard and tipped her glass to her lips for another taste of temptation.

He studied her carefully across the table. "Strange," he said, his voice wickedly low and raspy. "I never expected to find us allies of sorts."

"I feel we're more like . . . coconspirators."

One corner of his very desirable mouth

quirked up at that. "Whatever we are, I'm enjoying the alliance." He reached for her hand, the tips of his fingers making dangerous little circles against her palm. "Very much."

Fiona knew she should pull away. While she still could.

He was mesmerizing, his touch incendiary. She'd never met a man who could affect her so quickly, so overwhelmingly. She felt out of control. And control, she suspected, was something a woman could relinquish completely with Nick.

"Shouldn't we be discussing battle plans?" she asked, retrieving her hand from his.

"Mmmm. Yes, battle plans." He leaned back in his chair, relaxed, maddeningly devil-may-care. "Why don't I pick you up tomorrow . . . say around eleven and we'll, uh, plan maneuvers."

She wasn't at all sure she could trust this man's maneuvers. She could end up being the one under siege. She'd trusted another man once—Adam. Nearly marrying him. She didn't want to be a fool again.

"I suppose the sooner we come up with something, the sooner I can get back to Boston . . ."

He leaned forward across the table. "What waits for you back in Boston?" he asked. And who? he wanted to add, but refrained.

"My shop. When my father called me

about the wedding I only had time to stick a CLOSED sign in the front window."

"What kind of shop do you have?" He hoped what they said about curiosity was only true of cats.

"I sell antiques. Anything old and abandoned—from furniture, which I restore myself, to vintage jewelry."

When Nick thought of antiques he pictured rocking chairs and old bottles. But he suspected he'd find neither in her shop. Her eyes glowed just talking about it. He wondered if she knew that.

"And is this something from your shop?" he asked, feeling an overwhelming desire to touch the tiny emerald, set in a delicate old mounting, that hung around her neck. As his fingers touched the gem, nestling in the hollow of her throat, he saw her eyes flame with a brilliance that outdid the shimmering green of the stone.

Had it been a reaction to his touch?

Why did he fervently hope so?

Her fingers closed over his around the stone. Her voice was barely a whisper. "It was a piece from an estate sale. I couldn't bring myself to sell it."

"It suits you."

The fiery color belonged to her, and so did the unusualness of the mounting. Fiona Ames was as temptingly beautiful as the gem she wore.

He leaned closer, his hand still at her throat, intending only to brush his lips across the sweetness of hers. Once, only once. But she proved more of a threat than he thought. He wanted to savor and taste. He wanted to explore the nectar he found.

Gently, insistently, his tongue teased at her mouth, begging her lips to part and admit him, and when they did, softly, wantonly, he felt a sweet ache low in his body.

The touch of his kiss felt dangerous, Fiona thought as she leaned in for more of it, of him. He pulled back then, but only to trace her lower lip, outlining its fullness with the tip of his tongue until she thought she'd go mad.

His breath whispered across her lips like a caress, hot and inviting, arousing every tiny nerve ending in them. Then his mouth took hers again, more fiercely this time. She forgot time and place as emotions swirled around her. She could only taste and feel. Him. The rough demand of his mouth.

It was everything she'd imagined, yet like nothing she'd ever experienced before.

His hands found her face, cupping it, while he drew her deeper into the delicious contact. She should pull away, she knew, but she couldn't find the strength to stop this madness.

Then he drew back, the heat of his palms still on her face as he held her close. He let out a ragged sigh, then withdrew his hands, too. She was shuddering from the effects of the kiss. And so was he.

"I, uh, think I'd better get you back to your hotel," was all he could manage to say.

THREE

"How does Camille feel about her mother marrying?" Fiona asked Nick the following day.

For the past hour she'd been trying desperately to keep her focus on the problem they were supposed to be discussing. But ever since Nick had picked her up at the hotel, her mind kept getting derailed onto how stupendous last night's kiss on the starlit veranda had been.

"We can't count on any help from that corner, if that's what you're thinking," Nick replied. "Camille's always believed in letting people, including her mother, do their own thing. She does her own thing, tramping around the world, whenever and wherever the mood strikes her."

"A real free spirit, huh?"

"You got it."

Fiona huffed and puffed to keep up with Nick. She hadn't known the day's agenda would include a hike up the side of one of the mountains that ringed the city, but Nick claimed this was where he came whenever he had things to think about.

And today they had a knotty problem to think over, that was certain.

Fiona had dressed for the hot desert weather in a pair of yellow cropped pants and a scoop-neck top, not for the cool mountain air. But Nick had tossed a gray-striped sweatshirt at her, which she'd donned thankfully.

The thing fit her like a pup tent, hanging well below her rounded bottom, the sleeves dangling several inches past her wrists, but it was warm.

It also carried the scent of the man it belonged to. Clean and earthy and—sensual. Wearing something of his against her skin was equally sensual. Like putting on a lover's shirt after a night of slow, sultry sex. Not that she'd had a lot of actual experience in slipping into such apparel.

"Where is this place you're taking me?" she asked, nearly tripping over a rock in her path. She needed to keep her attention on where she was going instead of on the feel of Nick's clothing against her body.

Here Comes the Bride

"It's not much farther. Want to stop and rest?"

"I thought you'd never ask."

Fiona sank down onto a flat rock at the side of the trail. She was out of condition, she decided as her breath came in gasps.

Nick barely seemed winded. Either he was in great physical shape or he was part mountain goat. She couldn't fault his form, though, as he came to stand in front of her, looking as rugged as the terrain around him.

His dark brown hair glistened in the sunlight that slanted through the trees, and his eyes rivaled the blue of the sky overhead. His body was as hard as a tree trunk. A faded black Bally's sweatshirt stretched across his chest like a second skin, and a pair of well-worn khaki cutoffs hugged his legs.

"Drink?" he asked, handing her a bottle of Evian he'd tucked into a backpack for them.

"Yes, thanks." She took a swig, a small one, then handed him back the bottle.

She'd wanted more, but more would necessitate a trip behind a tree at some point in their hike, and she didn't want to go home with a case of poison ivy on her backside.

Okay, she was a city girl, through and through. She admitted that and wished they could have scheduled this planning session in a comfortable coffee shop—if Las Vegas had such a thing. So far all she'd seen were casinos and one very private bar.

Besides, of course, this uninhabited mountain.

When she didn't make any effort to get up and continue on, Nick borrowed a spot beside her on the rock. Their shoulders touched. Fiona sucked in a gulp of air. She had to get over the way this man affected her.

If it was body chemistry, it was explosive.

Not to mention, dangerous.

She stood up, feeling an overpowering need to put some distance between them. A sigh escaped her lips as she glanced up the tortuous trail that wound through a thicket of pine trees just ahead of them. "Ready to go?" she asked, trying to work enthusiasm into her voice.

"Ready," Nick replied, seeing she'd already begun hiking. He caught up to her in a few easy strides.

"Have you ever considered building a road up to this private spot of yours?" she asked, turning those big green eyes on him.

He'd spent the better part of last night trying to get her off his mind. The sweet taste of her mouth had bedeviled him into the worst sleepless night he'd endured in recent memory.

He'd tried to blame the restlessness on his concern for Winnie, but he damn well knew the root of the problem—one dynamite redhead who managed to look seductive even in his giant-sized sweatshirt.

The baggy garment didn't begin to hide her sensuality. It sizzled out of her with every wiggle as she picked her way up the rock-strewn path.

"A road would only bring all kinds of strange people up here, and then it wouldn't be very private, would it?" he answered, following behind her now that the trail had narrowed to single-file width.

He pinned his attention on the swing of her hair. She'd pulled it back and anchored it loosely with a stretchy bow, but that hadn't stopped its swish and bounce.

Last night, as he tried to get to sleep, one delicious fantasy about that hair had him thumping the feathers out of his pillow until morning. "Concentrate on that squirrel over there, Killian," he muttered.

"Did you say something?" She turned and glanced at him over her shoulder.

"I just said, 'Look at that squirrel over there.'"

She looked, unimpressed, at the furry creature. "This may come as a surprise to you, but I've seen squirrels before. We have them back East. Lots of them."

"Just pointing out the sights."

They hiked in silence for a while. Nick

trained his attention on the rocks and trees, anything but on the temptation in front of him. Spending the day with her had not been one of his better ideas. Spending it with her on the side of a mountain, in total isolation, bordered on the insane.

"Hang a right just past that gnarled pine," he said. They were there now, and he'd have to make the best of it. Come up with a plan fast, and get them the hell back down the mountainside.

Fiona turned where Nick indicated. She'd gone only a few steps when she came to a lofty rock perch that jutted out of the side of the mountain. Here the pine forest receded, allowing her an unobstructed view of the desert basin, shimmering like a mirage below them.

"What do you think?" Nick asked when she didn't speak.

It was easy to see why this was his favorite place to sort out life's problems. "It's beautiful, Nick." The words were woefully inadequate.

Small orange-and-yellow desert blooms eked life out of the rocks. The scent of pine was strong in the air. There was no sound except for the soft rustling of wind through the trees, an occasional bird, and Fiona's breathing, which hadn't yet slowed to normal from the hike up the mountain. Nick was so close beside her that she could almost hear the sure thudding of his heart and feel the heat of his skin.

She had the strong urge to turn and fold herself into his strength, to tip her head up and beg for one more of those kisses he'd devastated her with last night. But they had family matters to deal with, and the sooner they got to it, the better.

She picked out a spot on the rocky ledge and sat down. Nick did cooling-down exercises, stretching his gorgeous hamstrings in front of her.

Fiona tried to look past him at the picturesque view.

"If you're about through, we can get down to business," she snapped when she was finally at her wit's end—and about ready to drool.

"You should do some stretches so your muscles don't tighten up on you," he warned.

"If they do, you can carry me down the mountain. Now, I think we'd better start planning before the bride and groom are saying their vows."

"You're right." He picked a spot beside her on the ledge and parked his sexy buns.

"When is Camille expected to get here?" she asked, trying to gauge how much time they had to work with.

"Possibly late tonight or early tomorrow morning. She hadn't checked on flights yet."

"That soon?"

"She's in Bombay, not outer space."

Fiona frowned. Outer space would have suited their purpose better, she thought privately. "Then we've got to think of something fast, or the wedding will be on again before we know it."

Nick nodded and raised one eyebrow in thought.

Fiona did the same.

Nick came up with something first. "What if . . . Walter thought Auntie wanted him to sign those prenuptial papers?"

Her eyes widened. "But you said Winnie refused to ask him to sign."

"She did."

"Then how—"

"*I* show them to him."

Fiona shook her head. "Wouldn't work."

"Why not? You don't think he'd blow up, maybe call off the whole thing?"

"I think he'd go to Winnie about it, and when he found out this was your idea, not hers, your little trick would backfire." Fiona didn't mention that the idea of misleading her father and Winnie bothered her more than she cared to admit.

"Then you come up with something, since you're so brilliant," he said testily.

"That's what I'm trying to do." Fiona jumped up from the rock and paced back and forth in front of him. "Maybe we shouldn't be meddling in their lives," she said, feeling a sudden sense of guilt.

"I know. I have a few qualms about that myself," Nick admitted.

Fiona paced a few more lengths. "All I want is for my father to be happy, truly happy. How can he be sure about this marriage thing when they've only known each other—" She stopped and turned to look at Nick. "How long *have* they known each other?"

"I'm not sure, really. Three weeks, maybe four."

"That's all?"

Nick nodded. "Tops."

Fiona frowned and resumed her pacing. "What do they have in common? How can a relationship work when two people are so . . . well, *different?* Winnie's the flamboyant type. My father's more quiet. Not to mention set in his ways."

"Auntie too," Nick said. "It wouldn't work out between them, never in a million years."

"Right," she seconded wholeheartedly. "My father's lived all his life in the East . . . Boston. It's the only city he's known. He's only been out here a short while. In time he'll find he misses the seasons, the leaves turning gold in the fall, spring and the Red Sox games. . . ."

"And Auntie was raised in the West," Nick inserted. "She loves the desert, the year-round sunshine, the mountains a short drive away. This is just some crazy attraction between them. A temporary attraction."

"Exactly," Fiona agreed, then paused.

Something about this conversation bothered her. But she wasn't exactly sure what. She and Nick were in agreement, *perfect* agreement.

That was what she wanted, wasn't it?

Of course. She shrugged and turned to him. "So, now that we have that settled, what are we going to do about it?"

Nick dragged a hand through his hair. Fiona might have been talking about Walter and Winnie, but he was thinking in terms of Fiona and himself.

What about *their* differences, not to mention this unexplainable attraction between them?

The attraction part was dangerous, he knew that. So why did he have this overwhelming desire to find out if her lips tasted as sexy sweet as they had last night?

She'd stopped her agitated pacing and sank down on the ledge beside him again. The haunting scent of her flowery fragrance wafted around him, taunting his senses.

She was looking to him for an answer, her eyes wide and expectant, but he seemed to have forgotten the question. Ah, yes, the wedding. And their uncooperative relatives.

Here Comes the Bride

Fiona was waiting for him to come up with some gem of a plan, and he probably could do so, if only she wasn't sitting so close beside him, her lips pursed in a slight pout, provocative, taunting, tempting.

Hell, he wasn't ready to try for sainthood —and only a saint could resist the lure in front of him at this moment.

Her lips parted and Nick sucked in a breath.

In this situation he wouldn't even bet on the saint.

One taste, he thought, only one desperate taste, and then they'd get down to business.

He leaned closer and Fiona followed. He could feel her heat, her dangerous need that matched his own. Her scent bedeviled him, her parted lips enticed. With a low groan he claimed them, claimed her. She was softness and sweetness and fire in the desert.

But Fiona wasn't the kind of woman you kissed and then forgot, he realized as her mouth melted beneath his. She was the kind who got under a man's skin and stripped him of his sanity.

He felt his slipping inch by delicious inch.

Fiona could only emit a whimper as his kiss invaded her senses. She pressed her hands against his rock-solid chest, not to push him away, but to anchor herself to him before she floated off the edge of the mountain.

His arms slid around her, drawing her tighter against him. His lips tasted hot, sensually hot, as they explored hers, slowly, thoroughly, inviting every nerve ending she had into a fevered response. A soft moan of pleasure slid up her throat and purred onto her lips.

He murmured something, his voice a hoarse whisper, something hot and no doubt naughty. For the sake of her resolve she didn't want to know what it was.

His body was hard and demanding, and she didn't seem to have a spine's worth of willpower left in hers. She opened her mouth to him, and his tongue slipped inside, stroking, parrying the movements of her tongue. His hands didn't stay still, but caressed her back and up the sensitive sides of her rib cage, sending her body heat soaring.

She looped her arms around his neck, soaking up the feel of him, the strong corded muscles in his neck, the crisp ends of his hair as it curled over her fingers. She wanted to tangle them in its fullness and draw him closer into this kiss that she shouldn't be enjoying as much as she was. But she couldn't seem to stop herself.

She wanted it to go on forever—and then some.

But, with a frustrated groan, Fiona understood only too well. He drew back, only to return for one last nip of her lower lip as if he couldn't quite leave the taste of her. Her heart thudded heavily against her ribs, and she felt like all the air had fled from her lungs.

He trailed a finger over the tender underside of her chin. "I'm sorry," he said, his voice a rasp. "I seem to have a hard time keeping to the business at hand."

Fiona swallowed hard against the trail of heat his fingertip blazed against her skin. "In case you didn't notice, you weren't alone in that kiss."

"I noticed."

He watched as she stood, trying to compose herself. She walked to the edge of the mountain and studied the view. He fought down the urge to go to her, fold her into his arms once more, devour the taste of her.

But one kiss would never be enough to satisfy him. He knew that.

Fiona Ames was trouble, the kind of trouble he'd vowed to steer clear of since his marriage fell apart. The kind of trouble that could make him forget what the world was really like, the kind of world he saw in court on a daily basis.

"We're wrong for each other," she said so quietly he almost missed hearing her words. "As wrong for each other as Winnie and Walter."

She wasn't telling him anything he didn't already know. "I agree."

She continued looking out over the vista, her face averted from him. "All the objections we have about *their* relationship go double for us."

"Again, you're right."

"This is just some sort of . . . physical thing between us. . . . We're going to have to get past it."

"Easier said than done," he said half-aloud.

She turned around. "What?"

"I said, 'We can do that.'"

She studied him for a long, quiet moment, her green eyes unreadable. "Yes. Piece of cake."

Nick wouldn't go so far as to say that.

To forget Fiona he needed to stay far away from her, like two thirds of the country away. But she was here until the wedding—or until the wedding was off, whichever one came first.

Nick had to team up with her. Because of Winnie—because he owed it to his aunt not to let her make a mistake.

He didn't believe in love. He didn't believe in forevers. The world had taught him that early. When his mother died, when his father left. Left him for Winnie to raise. Winnie had been the only constant in his life. It was why he was so worried about her happiness, wanted it for her, but didn't believe it existed.

Fiona saw a fleeting shadow of pain in Nick's eyes, a hardness, and wondered what—or who—had put it there. His kiss had left her shaken, reeling. If she put a finger to her lips, she'd still find them quivering from the experience.

She didn't need to get involved with a man like Nick. She had the feeling he could cause heartache for any woman who was foolish enough to fall in love with him.

"Come on," he said gruffly, "let's start back down. Maybe we can think more clearly out of this rarefied air."

Fiona wasn't certain her legs would carry her back down the steep trail, but she agreed. They'd settled nothing up there at the top of creation, only stirred up something between them they shouldn't have.

The kiss they'd shared had been foolhardy. He'd made her want—and that was a risk she didn't dare take. She hadn't forgotten how much it had hurt to love another man—only to have that love destroyed.

She followed in Nick's wake, careful not to trip over exposed tree roots or half-buried rocks.

Neither of them spoke until they reached the four-wheel-drive Jeep they'd left where the road ended and the trail began.

Then Nick turned to her. "I've got it," he said. "The perfect plan."

Fiona raised a dubious eyebrow. "Oh? What is it?"

He helped her inside the Jeep, then slid in behind the wheel before he explained.

Fiona listened, played the devil's advocate for a while, then admitted she couldn't come up with anything better. "It just might work," she said.

His plan had only one major flaw—it would involve spending more time with Nick.

FOUR

Not ever again, Nick vowed. He wasn't riding with Walter ever again. He helped Winnie out of the backseat of the oldest living vehicle on the road as Walter discharged his passengers in front of the restaurant where the four of them were to have dinner that night.

"We're taking a taxi back," he whispered in Fiona's right ear as Walter gunned the huge sedan and peeled off to park it, a plume of blue smoke trailing from the exhaust. "I'm not setting foot in that tank again."

"Dad likes big cars. They make him feel secure," Fiona defended.

"Well, he could fight a war in that baby."

Fiona shot him a fierce glower. "If I remember right, this evening was your idea," she retorted, her voice low to keep Winnie from overhearing. "In fact, I believe the entire purpose of it was to get *them* arguing so they'd put off the wedding. So far, the only arguing I've heard is between *us*."

Nick frowned. He and Fiona scrapping like a pair of mad dogs was not in the plan. But neither was tonight's transportation snafu. How was he to know Walter would insist on doing the driving?

Just then there was a crunch of metal as Walter's old car came to rest against the stone retaining wall at the far end of the parking lot. Nick didn't hold out much hope for the wall standing up to the four-wheel battering ram.

Parking the thing himself was something else the man had insisted on; though, Nick had to admit, the valet had looked relieved when Walter refused his assistance. Nick couldn't blame the guy, who was probably accustomed to parking Jags and Rollses, and receiving hefty tips for the privilege.

"Nicholas, I think Walter may have hit something," Winnie said, tugging at Nick's arm. "Please go and check on him."

"I think he's fine, Auntie," Nick replied as Walter came loping into view a moment later.

"That wall got a little close," Walter said. "Knocked a chip or two of paint off the fender."

"Who cares about an old fender?" Winnie said. "It's you I'm worried about." She smoothed the lapels of his jacket and patted his chest. "Are you all right, Walter?"

"Ah, you were worried about me, Win?" He looked pleased at the possibility.

"I most certainly was."

Winnie linked her arm through his and they swept through the front door of the restaurant, oblivious to everything around them.

"So far this evening is a total failure," Fiona said, then started into the restaurant behind the couple.

Nick caught up to her just inside the doorway. "Have you got a better idea? If so, let's hear it."

He didn't know why he was as snappish as a crossed bear, even though the afternoon hadn't put him in a great mood. Touching Fiona, tasting her lips, feeling the press of her body against his had left him wanting.

Fiona had succinctly pointed out how wrong they were for each other. And they were. But that didn't mean spending the evening with her, in the company of Walter and Winnie, close but unable to touch, would be easy.

Unbearable. That was what it would be. Unbearable. And he had no choice but to endure it. Unless, of course, he wanted to see his aunt walk down that aisle with Walter.

"Are you coming?" Fiona asked, apparently choosing not to answer his barbed question.

She looked so damned tempting in that pale silk shirt and those matching pants that teased around her legs. Her hair was twisted into a French braid, a satin ribbon wound through it. Her scent was a whisper of something soft and feminine and threatening to his peace of mind.

"I'm right behind you," he said, and swallowed hard.

Right behind her meant watching the jiggle of her sexy backside as she strutted across the crowded restaurant behind Walter and Winnie.

As soon as they settled into their seats, the older couple decided they wanted a bottle of champagne to celebrate their upcoming nuptials.

When the waiter arrived with the bottle, Walter proposed a toast. "Here's to us and our new life together," he said, his eyes on his bride-to-be.

Nick frowned at the pair over the rim of his glass.

Fiona flashed him a do-something-or-else look.

He drummed his fingers on the table and somehow avoided her pointed stares until the food arrived.

As Walter aimed a morsel toward his

mouth Nick decided he'd light the evening's first stick of dynamite, hoping it would sizzle and explode like a bombshell.

"You know, Walter, that's going to be the last steak you enjoy in a *looong* while. Auntie will have you eating the stuff her health guru promotes."

That should do it, Nick thought. You didn't take a man's red meat away from him without provoking a war.

The older man frowned at Nick, then turned to Winnie. "Win just has my best interest at heart, don't you, sweet Win?"

The gaze of longing he bestowed on his intended was enough to give Nick indigestion.

"I just want to keep you young and virile," Winnie gushed back.

"Clever, Killian. Got any more brilliant ideas up your sleeve?" Fiona asked, leaning in close.

"No, but I'll think of something. I always do."

"Make it sooner rather than later."

"What are you two whispering about over there?" Winnie asked, directing her gaze across the table.

Nick and Fiona sat up straighter in their chairs.

"Nothing, Auntie," Nick replied. "Nothing at all." He shot Fiona a daggered look, his voice a low growl. "What are you trying to do? Blow this plan?"

"*What* plan?"

"*Our* plan—or have you forgotten we're in this thing together?"

What was the matter with her tonight? Fiona wondered. Nick was right; they were in this together. It was just that she was so worried about her father. That was all it was.

And maybe a little frustration thrown in.

Nick looked like a mixture of elegant and arrogant in his tux. And sexy. Her fingers itched to loosen that perfect black tie, work loose the pearl studs down the front of his pleated shirt, and . . .

Tonight was business. Underhanded business maybe, but business. She needed to keep herself focused—and not on Nick.

She decided to forgo dessert and watch while the others indulged. She alternated between telling herself the sinful-looking mousse was probably artificial tasteless chocolate and thinking up something that would precipitate an argument between their two dinner companions. She'd considered, then discarded, three ideas that were no better than what Nick had tried.

Across the table the soon-to-be newlyweds were spooning mousse into each other's mouths as if it were an aphrodisiac and whispering sweet nothings Fiona wasn't sure she wanted to hear. She shot a glance at Nick. He was scowling at the pair over his dessert. A smudge of dark chocolate clung to one corner of his mouth, and Fiona fought back the tempting urge to flick her tongue over it. The sexy corner of Nick's mouth was territory best left unexplored.

If this evening wasn't going to be a total nonevent, she needed to come up with something on her own, she decided.

She twisted her napkin in her lap for a moment before an idea came to mind, an idea that just might save the day—or rather, the night.

She cleared her thorat to gain her audience's attention. "Dad," she began, her voice deceptively innocent. "You'll never guess who I saw the other day."

"Who was that, Fiona?" Her father gave her a cursory glance then returned his gaze, along with a besotted smile, to Winnie.

Fiona tried to swallow the last of her guilt over what she was about to do, tried to convince herself it was for her father's own good. "Adele Winston," she said.

But her father wasn't listening. If she'd hoped the name of the lovely lady who came into the antique shop and often asked about Fiona's father would trigger a reaction, she'd been wrong.

But Nick was looking at her with a curious

glint in his eye. "Who is Adele Winston?" he demanded.

Fiona turned toward him. "Never mind. It doesn't matter."

He leaned close. "An old girlfriend. Is that what you're saying? Admit it—your father is a womanizer. What happened? Did Adele catch on to him before he led her to the altar?"

Fiona gasped at Nick's leap to a wrong conclusion. "He is not a womanizer. And no, Adele didn't catch on. . . . I mean . . ." She glanced across the table. Winnie and Walter weren't paying any attention to anyone around them. Certainly not to her and Nick. "I mean . . . I was going to make it up. As a part of *the scheme.*"

"And some scheme," Nick ground out. "I'll bet it works just great too."

She glanced across the table again. "*Our* scheme," she said, louder this time since the pair weren't listening, anyway.

But then, neither was Nick. His face told her he didn't believe a word of it. Fiona dropped her head into her hands and massaged her throbbing temples. This was one royal backfire. When she looked up again, Nick was staring across the table.

At nothing.

At no one.

The table was empty.

One moment Walter and Winnie were

holding hands and purring at each other, the next they'd disappeared, slipped away while she and Nick were arguing. Fiona turned back to Nick.

He shrugged. "Maybe it was something we said."

Fiona groaned. "This is all your fault. Now they've gone off to . . . to . . . to do heaven only knows what!" She wasn't ready to think about what that something might be.

Nick brushed away a springy curl that had slipped from her braid and teased at her cheek. "I could get into that."

Fiona sucked in a breath at the contact. "I think what we'd better do is come up with Plan B."

"This is not the lunch I had in mind. I apologize," Nick said as he watched Fiona fork the last of her Chinese takeout into her pretty mouth. "I hadn't planned to come into the office at all today, but Jasmine insisted this was a case that couldn't wait."

His secretary had told him the woman had called, distraught and crying. Nick was always a sucker for a lady in trouble. He supposed that was why he hadn't chucked his practice a long time ago and gone to work on dull, corporate cases.

Still, he wasn't sure how much more misery and suffering he could take without life warping him more than it already had.

Last night he and Fiona had agreed to meet for lunch today to map out Plan B. Nick had wanted to take her to his favorite Chinese restaurant, but after Jasmine had phoned about the tearful client, they'd had to settle for takeout.

"What kind of a case is it?" she asked, setting her empty container on the desk in front of her.

Nick tried hard not to notice how delectable she looked in her white, wrap-styled sundress. His gaze strayed to the tie closure at her narrow waist. One tug, he thought, one tug on those ties and the thing would come apart, revealing the prize underneath.

He raised his gaze back to her eyes. "Can't talk about it." He didn't want to talk about it, even if he could. For some strange reason he didn't want the sadder side of life he came up against daily to touch Fiona even slightly. "It's a divorce case. Ninety-nine percent of my practice is divorces."

Fiona nodded. She recalled her father telling her about Nick's law office. His practice was successful, according to what Winnie had told him. Judging from the seven secretaries in the front office, and the way Fiona sank into the expensively thick caramel-colored carpet as if ankle-deep in quicksand, Winnie hadn't exaggerated that success.

He'd introduced her to Jasmine, his personal secretary, a tall, leggy blonde, who seemed to adore her boss. The girl was friendly, and Fiona couldn't help but warm to her.

She had been a showgirl down on her luck in this hard town when Nick found her and gave her a job. Fiona had suspected Nick could play the tough courtroom lawyer—she'd seen the hard side of him more than once—but she began to believe there might be a mushy center as well to that encased heart of his.

Just then the intercom on his desk buzzed.

Nick stabbed a finger at the button. "Yes?" His tone was brisk, professional.

Jasmine's low, sultry voice came through. "Your appointment is here."

"Thanks, Jas."

Fiona stood up. "I'll, uh, get out of your way."

He slid his arms into the sleeves of the suit jacket that he'd taken off earlier and adjusted the knot on his tie. "Sit still. Jas will show her into the conference room. Make yourself at home."

With that he strode out of the room.

"Can I get you anything? Coffee? A soft

drink?" Jasmine poked her head in the door with a warm smile.

Fiona smiled back. "No, nothing, Jasmine. Thanks."

Fiona would have liked to talk with her, but she knew Jasmine was busy. She'd have liked to ask her more about Nick, the man behind the desk, the generous boss. The cynical man who held life at arm's length.

Fiona suspected the reasons he was opposed to this upcoming wedding were far different from the ones he voiced aloud.

What were they?

She paced the richly appointed office, fingering a lamp shade, a letter opener, a painting on the wall, as if one of them would give up the answer. His large cherrywood desk was piled high with work he'd no doubt put off in order to save his aunt from the fate of marriage to Fiona's father.

Amid the stack of legal papers and file folders was a framed picture. Fiona picked it up. It was a snapshot of Nick, his arm around two women. One of the women was Winnie, the recipient of Nick's warm gaze and all-too-infrequent smile.

It was true, she realized, a picture was worth a thousand words—or at least this one was. The photo had captured all the love Nick felt for his aunt Winnie, a rare and special kind of love.

Here Comes the Bride

Nick was a man of deep feelings—when he chose to show them. When he gave of himself it was completely, irrevocably. He asked nothing in return. Fiona thought of Jasmine. Nick had cared, given her a new start, and she obviously worshiped her boss for it. He loved Winnie with a fierceness that showed. For a moment she allowed herself to wonder what it would be like to be the one special woman in Nick's life. To experience the ferocity of his love.

A shiver ran down her spine.

She had no doubt that if he allowed himself to trust one woman enough, that would be the kind of love he would give.

Her gaze fell on the third person in the picture. The pretty face with the bright smile bore a strong resemblance to Winnie. It was the face of a woman who met life head-on, grasped at it with feverish excitement, much like Winnie did.

This was Camille, whom Fiona would meet tonight when her flight from India arrived.

Another evening with Nick—and her soon-to-be family.

His client had taken up more of his time than Nick had anticipated. But the meeting had been no different than he'd expected.

The woman had alternated between crying over her husband and threatening to surgically alter the man's body. For his misdeeds—of which she had a long list—she wanted a quick and ruthless divorce.

That was what they all wanted.

And what he got for them.

He tunneled a hand through his hair. Why, he wondered, couldn't two people realize they were ill suited *before* they exchanged marriage vows? Did love blind them to all the clues, their differences, their incompatibilities?

Wedded bliss didn't last, sometimes past the ink drying on the marriage certificate.

A legal pad of notes tucked under his arm, Nick headed for his private office, feeling an overwhelming need to see Fiona.

She stood at the window, gazing down at the street, the heat of the day shimmering off the pavement, the tops of the cars that shuttled by. At the sound of the door opening she spun around.

Nick stood in its frame, his blue eyes as dark as approaching dusk, his hair ruffled, as if he'd driven his fingers through its thickness.

Slowly he closed the door behind him, shutting out the hum from the outer office. She wanted to ask about the meeting, how it had gone, but her words stayed on her lips. Whatever had happened, it had taken the starch from him.

He stared at her for a long moment. She tried to read his eyes, his face, the set of his shoulders. He was a man besieged, bothered. A man hurting.

He crossed the room and dropped his legal pad onto the desk, then came to stand in front of her. His arms went around her and he held her to him. Just held her.

She could feel the tremor in his body and she wanted to say something soothing, but before she could, his mouth found hers in a possessive kiss, a needful kiss, a taking kiss.

Instinctively Fiona gave. She crushed him to her, letting his mouth plunder, returning the hot thrust of his tongue. Her hands stroked him, caressed him, drawing him closer for warmth, for the solace he seemed to need.

She felt the tension in his shoulders, the strong column of his neck. His heart thundered against her breasts, and her own raced in rhythm. His hands tangled in her hair, his fingertips pressing into her scalp. They made hot circles against her back, her arms, touching every inch of her as if to assure himself that she was real, that she wasn't going to disappear in a breathless moment.

His touch sent a languid heat seeping through every fiber of her until she wasn't able to give, only take, take more of his kiss, his heat, his hands.

Greedily.

Nick had vowed to keep hands off, but he'd needed to feel Fiona's soft body against his; he'd needed to seek out her sweetness; he'd needed her solace before he lost his sanity.

But Fiona offered her own brand of insanity, the kind that stole all thought from a man's brain, the kind that made him forget everything but this moment, an incredible moment out of time, a moment of stolen peace.

She made him forget, at least for a time, the horrors of bad marriages, of failed relationships.

He only felt the sweet heat of her mouth that he wanted to possess, the softness of her breasts as they pushed against him, the pliant curves of her body pressed to his. She was heat and fire and tempting madness.

She gave what he needed, with no question, as if she understood his pain. But he couldn't take from her, couldn't violate her sweetness unless he could give of himself.

And he had nothing to give.

With a muffled groan of regret, he tore himself away from the succor of her lips, away from the warmth of her body.

"Fiona . . ." He had to say her name, had to hear it hum on the air.

"What, Nick?"

He touched her cheek, red with the heat of desire. His fingers trembled on her face as they trailed over the velvet of her skin. Was she asking why he spoke her name? Or why he hurt?

He didn't want to answer either.

He grasped her hand. "Let's get out of here."

FIVE

Nick drove across the hot desert as if demons were chasing him. Fiona glanced at him. His posture was as unrelenting as the hard landscape they drove through, his jaw tense, the backs of his hands corded as they gripped the wheel.

"I think I understand, Nick," she said quietly beside him.

He glanced over at her. "Understand what?"

"Why you suggested that prenuptial agreement to Winnie. Why you're against the wedding—the real reason."

Nick turned his gaze back to the road. He saw in her eyes that she did glimpse—at least in part—what ate at his soul. His jaded mistrust. Of marriage. Of love.

"I see a lot of divorces, Fiona. None of them are pretty."

"Not all marriages end up in court," she returned. "My parents' marriage didn't. They were happy, blissfully happy, for thirty years."

Nick gave her a stony look. "They were the exception, Fiona."

Marriage was a farce. For better or worse, they all promised. The *better* part was easy, but few stuck around for the *worse*. He knew that. His own marriage hadn't lasted out a year.

He supposed, in all truth, he had to take most of the blame for its failure. His disillusionment had begun to show by then, his disillusion with love, caused by the unending parade of divorce cases that came through his office, the failed relationships.

It had colored his world, warped his viewpoint and eventually his marriage to Catherine. She had failed to see he was hurting—and he hadn't known how to tell her.

He'd hurt from the time his mother died. His father hadn't cared to stick around. Jake Killian had licked his wounds by nursing a stiff drink, until finally he'd walked away from his son and never looked back.

Maybe Jake had known what Nick came to learn later: Stay away from serious entanglements. They rendered a man vulnerable.

He turned to glance at Fiona. Especially

Here Comes the Bride

entanglements with women who believed in hearts and flowers and matches made in heaven.

"You love your aunt very much, don't you?" Fiona said softly. She had seen that love shining in Nick's eyes, had sensed his fierce protectiveness toward Winnie more than once.

"Auntie raised me like her own son after my mother died," he said. And Uncle Gray stood in as father to a lonely little boy, he thought privately. He shrugged aside the memory.

Fiona wanted to offer sympathy, but sensed somehow that Nick wouldn't accept it. She knew what it was like to lose a mother. "How old were you then?"

"Eight. Winnie and Gray were wonderful to me. They saw I had everything growing up. They put me through college, then law school. A few years ago Gray died, but before he did, I promised him I'd look after Auntie. Protect her and her interests."

Protect her from men like Fiona's father, Fiona thought with a small, private smile. But she had to admire Nick for his devotion to the family he loved, for offering to look after his aunt. But soon that task would fall to her father. She wondered how Nick would react to that. Would he relinquish responsibility gracefully once Winnie was married?

"It sounds like Gray loved her very much," she said, returning her thoughts to their conversation.

Nick's face showed the hint of a smile, the first she'd seen this afternoon. "Yes," he said quietly. "They were very happy."

"Another example of a marriage that lasted," she felt compelled to point out, but wasn't sure if it was for Nick's sake or to reassure herself that it was possible, just possible, that marriage could work a second time. For her father. For Winnie.

Nick frowned over at her. "I said there were rare exceptions. Maybe it was because they'd known each other so well, and for so long. Auntie told me they'd been childhood sweethearts."

His reply didn't reassure her.

He grew silent then, withdrawing into his thoughts. She wanted to ask him more about himself, about his mother, the father he hadn't mentioned, but she somehow sensed that this was an area where her probing questions wouldn't be welcome.

She dragged her gaze away from him and turned it on the passing scenery, the bleached landscape, the struggling vegetation, the dust devils kicking up here and there across the desert floor.

That was what she felt like inside—a dust devil, whirling madly around. Emotionally.

Nick had reached into her heart and touched her on some level she hadn't been fully aware of. She wasn't sure she should respond. Feeling anything for Nick Killian could be dangerous.

"They're miniature tornadoes," Nick said, seeing Fiona studying the strange desert phenomenon. They'd always intrigued him and he'd even done a project for a science fair when he was in school, analyzing then re-creating the activity.

"The kind that can't hurt you, I hope," she replied.

"They won't hurt you, Fiona." Nick turned his gaze back to the road ahead. He didn't know where he was headed; he was just driving. Eating up miles.

He and Fiona were supposed to be plotting the demise of their relatives' wedding plans, but the wedding seemed fated to take place, despite any attempt on their part to delay it.

Maybe he should just enjoy the day with Fiona. She'd be out of his life soon enough.

Yes, he would enjoy the day with her, come what may.

Then suddenly he knew where he wanted to take her. "There's a place I want you to see," he said. "It's only a short drive from here. Are you game?"

Fiona didn't know what she was promising, but she nodded. "I'm game."

A lizard ran across her feet and Fiona squealed. But despite a few unwanted denizens the town offered, she was delighted they'd come.

Surprise, Nevada. A place time forgot.

A page out of the Old West.

The ghost town seemed lost in the desert. As different from the bright lights of Las Vegas as anything could get.

Feeling like she was on some kind of busman's holiday, she stepped into a dusty antique shop and soaked up the atmosphere. Her eyes couldn't take everything in fast enough. She gripped Nick's arm, her fingers tightening around his biceps, as if for support.

"Oh, Nick, you knew I'd enjoy this."

Nick smiled. The name of the town, Surprise, couldn't begin to compare with the look of surprise shining in Fiona's eyes when they'd reached their destination. It had been an expression he would remember long after she'd gone back to Boston, an expression he would cherish.

"Go on," he said. "Look around."

Fiona released his arm and went to peer into a locked glass case, full of artifacts and treasures from a bygone era. "The inhabitants lived well," she said.

"The gold they mined around here made people millionaires overnight," Nick replied, and leaned in next to her to see what it was that had caught her eye.

"Then just like that, their wealth was gone again," she said sadly, remembering what she'd learned in history class years before.

She was looking at bits and pieces of people's lives, at dreams gone bust. In a twinkling. It made her want to reach out and hold on to life with both hands and never let go.

It was a feeling she often got when she acquired a prized antique for her shop, but it struck her even more strongly out here in the desert. Perhaps because she felt she was losing her father.

Perhaps because of Nick, a man she'd be walking away from in a few short days, a man she'd probably only see again occasionally when the two families met at Christmas or Thanksgiving.

Nick saw something flit across Fiona's face and wondered what she was thinking about, but then her eyes brightened again as she moved on to a display of old dishes. He watched as she fingered a goblet, traced the gilt edge on a fancy plate.

He picked up a dusty purple bottle of dubious value and held it up to the light, wondering what anyone saw in all this junk.

What Fiona saw in it.

Shards of light filtered through the bottle, fanning out in prisms of purplish hues. Kinda pretty, he thought, but then so were sunsets.

So was sunlight shining through Fiona's fiery hair.

He set the bottle down with an unceremonious thunk. If anyone had told him a few short days ago that he'd be wandering through an antique store and musing about sunsets and a woman with tempting red hair that he'd only just met, he'd have laughed.

Raucously.

Still, the alluring sight of her bending over to touch a filigree trinket propelled him across the room. He slid in next to her and fitted his hand to the curve of her firm derriere just below her waist. The flowery fragrance of her special perfume sent him into a spiral of desire. Unadulterated want.

He'd never known another woman who could turn him on with just a look, a smile, a twist of her body, the way Fiona could. She glanced up then, her green eyes wide and expectant, and straightened to her full height. His hand slipped to a less intimate position at her waist.

She still held the trinket in her hand, a gilt bauble with old gemstones set in it—gemstones as glittery as the lights shining in her eyes at that moment.

"What do you have there?" he asked, hoping his voice didn't betray the turmoil inside him.

"Oh, Nick, it's a lady's jewelry box. Old, delicate, tiny. I thought it was brass when I first saw it, but it's gold." Her hand touched it reverently.

The piece was ornate, a remnant of better times, when gold ran like a river through this desert, Nick thought. And he wanted Fiona to have it. Because she admired it. Because it brought a smile to her lips just gazing at it. And her smile was something he couldn't seem to get enough of lately.

She whirled around in a sweeping gesture. "I'd like to buy all this and ship it back to my shop. Each antique is so unusual, at least compared with what I find in New England. It would sell well."

"Including the jewelry box?"

She fingered a curlicue on the top of it. "This I wouldn't sell." She set it down gingerly.

While she was busy trying to figure out how an old miner's sluice worked, Nick slipped the clerk the money for the tiny jewelry box and hoped Fiona didn't return for another glance at it and find it missing.

Buying the antique bauble for her felt good. Strangely good.

He didn't want to ponder why.

"Let's stop at the Gold Slipper for a cool drink," he said when she'd checked out every nook and cranny of her third antique shop in a single block.

When they were seated in the red-and-gilt room off the lobby of the old town's restored hotel, sipping icy lemonades, he set the small filigree box in front of her. "For you," he said simply.

Her eyes widened. "You . . . you bought it?"

"I wanted you to have it."

"But . . ." Her gaze diverted from the small jeweled square to his face. "Oh, Nick, I —I can't accept this. It's too valuable."

"It was too valuable to leave there for someone else to buy, Fiona, someone who wouldn't appreciate it the way you would."

"That's not fair, Nick. To put it that way." A way he knew would get to her, appeal to her sentimental side. How had he known that was her weakness? She often bought antiques she knew she couldn't afford—and would never want to resell—just because she couldn't bear to have them go to some grasping dealer.

She ran the tip of one finger gently over the box, knowing this was one time she should be strong. She and Nick were two people who'd been brought together by a strange quirk of fate, nothing else. And to accept such a gift implied more.

She drew her eyes from the small trinket and looked up at him, her lips ready with a firm no, but he was smiling, a pleased-as-punch grin, and she couldn't do it.

Nick was a puzzle to her. One moment he was as tough as an old miner's boot, and the next he was— She decided not to finish that thought. It would be better to think of him as a tough miner's boot than someone warm and— Skip that thought, too.

She was beginning to care entirely too much about Nick Killian. And that was not good. She'd only known him a few days. And in another few days she'd be out of his life, back in her own world.

For now she would accept his gift graciously. And perhaps later she could find a way to repay him. "Thank you. I know just the spot in my apartment where this will go."

"Ah, where?"

"I have this big rosewood four-poster, something I bought to resell then couldn't bring myself to part with. I'm going to set this on the night table beside it."

"Beside your bed?"

"Yes."

Why did the word *bed* falling from Nick's lips sound so intimate? Fiona swallowed hard and glanced away from the heat she saw in his eyes. It had been an innocent remark, but now it seemed far from that.

Nick glimpsed the sudden rise of color in Fiona's cheeks. He wanted to see them heat like that in the throes of passion. He wanted to make love to her in that big four-poster, her flame-red hair spilled across the pillow. Wild love. Slow, thorough love.

A pulse point beat in her neck and he wanted to lean in close and kiss it. He wanted to sample every inch of her skin, taste its silken heat.

Damn, what was this woman doing to him?

He didn't even know himself anymore. She had him acting erratically, rambling through old stores, perusing purple bottles, and wanting to know every little thing about her life.

"So, where do you find stuff like big rosewood four-posters?" he asked. He'd rather ask what she wore at night when she slipped between its covers, but decided it was better that he didn't know. "Do you prowl around old dusty shops, go to sales, what?"

"I keep my eye open for any possibility," she said. "I scour the newspapers for estate sales. I go on buying jaunts through every tiny burg within a hundred-mile radius of Boston.

Sometimes I travel farther afield, wherever I get the whiff of a good sale."

"Like a bloodhound?"

She laughed and Nick loved the sound. It trickled up from her throat, more beautiful than the ripple of water purling over smooth stones in a brook.

"It takes a lot of hours to find the special things my customers will want, restore them to their original beauty, whether wood or pewter or brass, and still keep shop hours."

"What do you do with your spare time?" He wondered what filled it, who filled it.

"What spare time? I trek around the countryside on Sundays and Mondays. At night I polish and stain. Tuesdays through Saturdays I'm busy with customers, if I'm lucky."

He took her hand and turned it over, looking for calluses. A few had tried to mar the softness of her palms. He traced the edge of one gently with his fingertip, then lifted her hand and kissed the spot.

Her hand softened under the press of his lips, and when he glanced up into her face, he saw her eyes had dilated perceptibly. A small smile curved at her mouth and the pink blush on her cheeks turned a pretty rose.

He was glad he could affect her like that. "Why don't you take on a partner?"

It took her a moment to speak, as if she needed to gather her wits. Or maybe her voice. "A partner?" There was a slight trembling to her words. "My shop's small and struggling. There's hardly enough income for one person. Maybe in another year or two I could hire an assistant, at least part-time."

"You love your work, don't you?" He didn't release her hand, just stroked it absently, tracing the tinge of a faint blue vein under her alabaster skin.

Her voice trembled again. "I must be boring you."

"Not at all. I want to hear more. What you do for fun, what you do for . . . love."

Her eyes widened, then narrowed slyly. "If that's your unsubtle way of asking if there's a man in my life, there isn't one at present."

That was what he was asking—and the answer pleased him enormously. He couldn't stop the smile that revealed his pleasure.

"There was someone once," she continued. "Someone I thought I knew, then found out I didn't. Fortunately before I married him."

"Is that why you believe in being cautious?"

She withdrew her hand from his and dropped it into her lap, her gaze lowered. He much preferred to feel her looking at him, caressing his face in that way she was unaware of.

She nodded. "I thought love could happen

overnight, but . . . it doesn't. At least if it does, it doesn't last."

"That's why you want your father to wait rather than jump into a marriage with Auntie?"

Her eyes raised. They were solemn and wide. And sad.

"What happened, Fiona? With this man you thought you knew?" Nick hated the bastard. Would string him up by some tender part of his anatomy if he could. For what he'd done to her.

Fiona drew in a ragged breath. She hadn't thought about Adam in a long time, hadn't wanted to, yet she supposed Nick was right, her experience with Adam had made her cautious. It was why she didn't believe in love at first sight, not for her father and Winnie, and certainly not for herself.

Love at first sight was merely lust in disguise, the purely physical attraction she felt for Nick being a prime example. Still, she'd never felt anything this strong, this overwhelming, this powerful with Adam. With any man. And she wasn't sure how to gird herself against it.

"It was a long time ago, Nick. I was very young. It doesn't matter now, anyway."

"Are you sure, Fiona?"

"I'm sure."

She didn't want to tell Nick what a little

fool she'd been, that she'd misread Adam so completely, so stupidly. That she hadn't recognized sooner that the man didn't have a faithful bone in his body, that he'd come on to some of her friends, that he'd even had a reckless affair with one of them.

It had been painful for her when she'd learned of his betrayal, but now it was merely embarrassing. She'd refused to suffer that pain for long, had refused to waste the emotion on a man who wasn't worth her time or energy.

But she knew Nick was right, the lesson she'd learned affected her today, colored her world, her belief system.

She didn't want Nick's sympathy, didn't need him charging up on his white steed to save her from some old hurt, from some man who'd wronged her. "Come on, Nick, let's go and watch the street entertainers."

SIX

"Hurry, we're going to be late."

Nick raced through the airport, Fiona panting along behind him. She didn't want to do this, she didn't want to meet Camille. If the woman was on this flight as Nick expected her to be, the wedding would be on again all too soon.

But Nick wasn't offering her much choice. His long legs carried him down the concourse. She had to hurry to keep up.

Part of her was still back in Surprise, back in the idyll of their afternoon together. She didn't want to be dragged back into the present—and the set of worries she'd temporarily put aside.

The plane was already discharging its passengers by the time they reached the gate area. Nick grabbed her hand and searched the crowd for a glimpse of his cousin.

"Maybe she didn't make the flight. Maybe she missed her connection in New York," Fiona said.

It was a hopeful wish, she knew, but a wish that would only put off the inevitable. Camille would be on this flight, or the next, if she missed this one.

"There she is."

"Where?"

Nick didn't answer, only boomed, "*Camille!*"

Fiona's gaze threaded through the crowd to see which one of the milling passengers he was calling to. And then she saw her, recognizing her immediately from the picture on Nick's desk.

"Nick!" Camille had spotted him, too, and waved.

Camille seemed to have stepped out of another era. Fiona smiled at the aura of the perennial flower child she projected in her loosely flowing skirts and her Birkenstocks.

Her hair—long, dark tresses—trailed down to the curve of her derriere. Three travel-battered duffels hung from one thin shoulder. Other than the hint of a little jet lag, she had a lively face, full of emotion and feeling.

And Fiona knew she liked her.

It would be hard not to like Camille.

"Am I too late?" Camille asked, wrapping her arms around Nick in a giant hug. "Did they do it, did they have the wedding without me?"

"No, they didn't," Nick assured her. "You wanted them to wait, and they did."

She sighed in relief, then turned her smile on Fiona. "Hello, sister," she said in a greeting that caught Fiona a little off guard.

Sisters? That's exactly what this wedding would make them, Fiona realized with a start. But Camille's warmth was undeniable.

"Hello, Camille," she said, then they hugged like they were already family.

Nick shouldered his cousin's bags. "Is this all or do we need to stop by baggage claim?"

"This is it."

Camille linked one arm through Nick's, the other through Fiona's, smiling first at one then the other.

Their walk to the parking garage where Nick had left the car led them past the very baggage carousel where Fiona's misadventure had begun. Had it been only a few short days ago?

"You were smart to carry your own bags," Nick said. "These things are rough on them." He indicated the spinning silver monster that had nearly mulched his wicked pieces of underwear. "Remind me to tell you about it, cuz."

"Oh? Is this something I should know about?" Camille was instantly curious.

He exchanged a look with Fiona, one only the two of them could share.

"Let's just say Nick had an intimate encounter with the thing," Fiona remarked.

"I want to hear about this," Camille said, intrigued.

But the story would have to wait. Nick escorted the two women into the garage and Auntie's Mercedes parked nearby. Winnie and Walter had wanted to be part of the welcoming committee, too, but Nick couldn't be sure Walter wouldn't insist on driving. He'd left the pair at Auntie's, blowing up bright "welcome home" balloons for Camille.

Nick would like to skip the small impromptu party they had planned and spend tonight alone with Fiona. He'd enjoyed this afternoon with her. Very much. He hated reality intruding, the reality of this wedding that he knew his little cuz would be all for.

She and Auntie would have their heads together the minute she got there, plotting and planning down to the last orange blossom.

Maybe he could get Camille alone for a moment, for a small family discussion, and make her see this matrimonial idea of Auntie's for what it was—one big mistake.

It was worth a shot, he thought, but given the fact that Camille saw the world through rose-colored glasses, he wasn't holding out much hope of making her see reason.

Maybe Fiona had the best idea after all. Set them down and talk turkey to them—each separately, of course. Together they tended to gaze besottedly at each other—and no amount of reasoning could win out over that.

He glanced over at the two women as he made his way out of the parking garage and onto the airport road. Camille was relating some wild adventure about how she'd slept on the luggage rack in a train car and eaten biscuits out of a knapsack while she traveled into India's remotest regions.

Fiona was listening raptly. Every time he looked at her he remembered this afternoon, the reverence in her eyes when she'd touched the small jewelry box, the look of disbelief on her face when she realized he'd bought it for her. He'd never been in the habit of giving such gifts to the women who passed through his life, but Fiona was different. Fiona was special. He wished that realization didn't strike such terror into him.

But it did.

He caught Fiona's soft laugh of amusement at something his cousin had said. What, he didn't know. He was content merely to listen.

The traffic was unusually light on Sahara for this time of day. He leaned back into the Mercedes's soft, plush leather, one arm draped over the wheel, while he breathed in Fiona's hypnotic scent. She was muddling his mind, overloading his senses—and he didn't know what the hell he was going to do about it.

He didn't know what the hell he was going to do about *her*.

By the time they reached Auntie's, the two women were fast friends, leaving Nick feeling like the uninvited guest at a wedding.

A poor pun, he thought with an agonized groan.

Furthermore, he didn't like feeling unessential in Fiona's life. It was a petty emotion and one that surprised him.

The woman was usurping too much of his peace of mind.

Everyone was gathered around the pool when they got there. Camille gave appropriate responses over the balloons tethered to everything stationary, and hugged Walter, already accepting the fact that he would soon be part of her mother's life.

Auntie had invited half of Las Vegas's permanent population, it seemed. Guests milled around everywhere. Nick avoided them, hovering by a potted palm, and quietly sipped his drink.

Fiona was being duly presented to friends,

old and new. He watched her move gracefully through the crowd, her hair shimmering a glorious russet under the patio lights. It brushed the tops of her creamy shoulders, left bare by the shirred top of her iris-colored dress.

Only two tiny straps kept the dress decent, he realized as his imagination played with the idea of sliding them down her arms.

He'd undress her slowly, very slowly, until he could feast his eyes on every lovely inch of her. Their lovemaking would be fevered and fierce, then they'd play it out again. This time he'd take his time, the way it ought to be. He'd dreamed of making love to her, perhaps from the first moment he'd laid eyes on her.

"She's beautiful, cousin," Camille said, apparently having escaped the group to come and interrupt his parade of thoughts.

"Who?" he asked, feigning innocence.

"The woman you haven't been able to take your eyes off of all evening."

He took a hard swallow of his bourbon, the ice cubes clinking against his teeth. "Camille, you've been out in the sun too long."

"Oh, you're smitten, all right. I noticed it right off."

"How clever of you." Nick didn't intend to give an inch. "I think instead of observing my love interest, you need to consider your mother's."

Camille raised an eyebrow. "Walter? He's precious. And perfect for her."

"Somehow I thought you'd say that."

"You don't approve of this wedding, do you?"

Nick snorted. "Definitely not."

"Might I ask why?"

"It'll be all over within six months, and then Auntie will be brokenhearted. And very possibly broke as well. She wouldn't ask Walter to sign that prenuptial agreement I drew up."

"Bully for Mother!" Camille's eyes narrowed. "And she should fire you as her attorney for even suggesting it."

He groaned. He was three for three. Three women who opposed his very practical suggestion. Auntie, Fiona, and now Camille. Seemed to be a trait of females.

There were any number of clients in his practice who'd have been better off today if they'd only thought ahead. He frowned. "Fire me for caring? Looking out after her?"

Camille stabbed a finger at his hard chest. "Walter will be doing that from now on."

Nick finished off his drink in one big gulp, then stared morosely into the ice at the bottom of it. "Yeah—Walter."

"What's that supposed to mean?" She didn't wait for his answer, just launched into a list of the man's virtues.

There was only one that held any water as far as Nick was concerned—he was Fiona's father. The man couldn't be all bad.

"I think I need another drink," he said.

"And I want to talk to Fiona." Camille smiled smugly. "Since you won't tell me what's going on between the two of you, maybe she will."

"There's nothing going on."

"Yeah, and I'm the queen of India."

Fiona glanced around the patio and caught sight of Nick frowning at his cousin. They were clearly arguing about something. And it didn't take much to guess what it was. The wedding.

She turned back to the couple she'd been talking with, old friends of Winnie's—Madge and Sol. Or was it Midge and Sal? She couldn't remember. She couldn't remember half the people she'd been introduced to and was wishing she could escape.

Just then Camille interrupted. "Excuse us a moment, Madge, Sal. I need to talk to Fiona." She spirited Fiona away from the couple, toward an umbrella-topped table at the edge of the pool.

Whatever it was she and Nick had been arguing about seemed to have been forgotten. Camille's blue eyes were bright, smiling.

Fiona pulled out a white pool chair and sat down across from Camille, happy to give her feet a respite.

"So, are you meeting everyone?" Camille asked, tucking a strand of her long, dark hair behind one ear. "Mother's friends can be daunting sometimes."

Fiona slipped her toes out of one shoe and wriggled them. "Let's just say I'm glad for a break."

"Good. I thought we could talk."

Fiona cupped her chin in one hand, wondering if Camille was here to woo her over to her side in the argument she and Nick had been having. She let her glance stray across the patio to Nick. His gaze was on her, hot and silky, then with a half smile, he saluted her with his drink.

She wanted to get better acquainted with Camille, but a part of her wanted to slip across the patio and into Nick's arms, feel his warm breath against her cheek. She'd enjoyed their closeness this afternoon; she yearned for it now.

"Fiona, Nick doesn't approve of this wedding. I need to know how you feel about it."

Camille's words drew her back to the present in a very real way, back to the reason she was here—her father's and Winnie's intended nuptials, not Nick and being with him.

She was losing her focus. Nick was doing that to her. "How do *I* feel about it?"

"Yes. Are you for or against this marriage?"

Fiona studied Camille's earnest face. She didn't want to say anything against Winnie. She liked Winnie. It was just that she wasn't convinced her father and Winnie knew each other well enough to take such a serious step. "Camille, I'm going to be honest with you."

"Good. I want you to be. I've been gone for a year and a half. I don't know what's really been going on in Mother's life."

Fiona leaned forward. "I'm not sure I do either—in my father's life, that is. This wedding came as a total surprise to me. And I haven't had much of a chance to adjust to the idea."

She didn't add that Nick kept her too off balance to think, to search out her deeper feelings. "Camille, I'm not against the wedding, at least not completely. I guess what I'm worried about most is that they haven't known each other long enough to take this step."

She thought back to her conversation with Nick that afternoon and what she'd told him about her near disaster with Adam. Had she jumped into a hasty marriage with him, she'd have let herself in for a whole lot of heartache.

She didn't want that for her father. Or for Winnie.

"But they seem so happy," Camille protested. "Look at them."

Fiona's glance followed Camille's to the couple. Winnie was talking animatedly to the small group that had gathered around them.

Winnie was clearly holding court, wrapped in a swirl of iridescent-colored silk. Her dark hair, streaked with silver, was fashioned into a twist at the side of her head and studded with a bright feather that looked like it had just been plucked from an unsuspecting peacock.

Fiona turned back to Camille. "My mother was a very different kind of person than Winnie is," she said softly, remembering the woman who had nurtured and loved her, the woman she still missed very much. "She was warm and sweet—not that Winnie isn't," she added hurriedly. "But in a different way entirely."

"You mean, she baked cookies," Camille interjected. "I grew up thinking cookies came out of a cellophane package." She paused, smiling. "You're very lucky, you know. Mother kept things lively around here, but I often wondered what it would be like to have a mom who headed up the Brownie troop, instead of one who made Auntie Mame seem tame."

Fiona laughed. She guessed she was very lucky. She'd never wished for something other than the childhood she'd had.

Here Comes the Bride

was the first time all evening she hadn't been sensually aware of his location, and she'd nearly collided with him. She had Camille to thank for that.

She didn't want to think what Nick Killian meant to her, how he had begun to affect her life. She wanted to forget that drink she'd come after and get out of there instead. "Is it possible to sneak away from one of these little soirees of Winnie's?"

Nick gave her a wicked grin. "I thought you'd never ask."

Fiona wanted to go back to her hotel, indulge in a long shower, and crawl into bed. She wanted to forget about this wedding and forget about Nick. But from the look on his face, he had something else in mind.

The thought of sliding between the covers with Nick sent her pulse pounding. Her throat went dry. And the desert breeze that had cooled her all evening seemed to have heated up into a furnace blast. She was certain her cheeks were fire-hot just thinking about what this man could do to her body.

She banished the thought and gathered her wits. "That's not what I meant. Besides, you can't leave—Winnie's counting on you."

He glanced toward Winnie, her hand on Walter's arm as they chatted easily with a clutch of friends. "They'll never miss us," he said.

"What about Camille? This is her first night home."

"She won't miss us either."

"Wanna bet?" The words slipped from Fiona's mouth and she regretted them the moment Nick's brow rose curiously.

"Oh?" His monosyllabic reply was a question.

Fiona frowned. "If we leave, she'll draw conclusions about us."

Nick smiled, a smile similar to the one he'd worn the first time she saw him, surrounded by a bevy of interested females at the baggage carousel as he gathered up his undies. "What conclusion might that be?"

"The, uh, obvious." She brushed the air with her hand, hoping that answer would put a stop to his growing amusement.

It didn't.

"The obvious? You mean that we're sneaking away to make hot, passionate love together?"

"She could draw that conclusion."

Fiona didn't like this conversation and wished she could start it over. She'd damn well make sure it came out differently. She'd say something glib, something casual, something that couldn't be misinterpreted.

"Maybe we shouldn't let a good conclusion go to waste."

He teased a wisp of her hair that blew

across her fevered cheek, and Fiona sucked in a breath at his touch, the intimacy of the gesture further heightening her feelings.

The image of sliding between the sheets with Nick returned full force, swamping her senses, firing them to a heated pitch. His nearness was overpowering. The velvet torture of his words wafted on the air, full of dangerous promise.

Succumbing to Nick was a very palpable threat, one she doubted she had the strength to fight. Or the will. "Nick, I—"

Fiona never knew what she was about to say because at that moment everyone's attention was drawn to Winnie and her father.

Winnie clapped her hands for quiet. She wanted to make an announcement.

"Uh-oh," Nick uttered beside Fiona.

"What do you mean, 'uh-oh'?"

As Winnie began to speak Fiona realized fully what he meant. Winnie glowed, her cheeks adazzle with color, her eyes soft, her smile wide and excited.

"Boys and girls, friends and family," she said, smiling out over the party. "Walter and I want you to know that our little wedding that had been postponed is on again."

A rush of murmurs went through the gathering. Beside her, Nick groaned, a sound Fiona felt all the way to the deepest part of her. She reached for his hand. He squeezed it in his, his palm hot against hers, his fingers laced through her fingers, until she felt bound to him.

They were together in this, she realized. The only two against the group of happy well-wishers, two reeds in the wind—and they didn't stand a chance.

Winnie went on. "You are all invited to come and help us celebrate this special occasion. Day after tomorrow. Six o'clock in the evening." She turned to Walter and pecked him on the cheek, one quick kiss before they were deluged with congratulatory wishes.

SEVEN

"Well, I guess there's nothing left to do but break out my tux," Nick said as he paced the length of the white-latticed gazebo.

"And I'll have to shake the wrinkles out of the pink linen suit I'd hoped I wouldn't have to unpack," Fiona returned. She sat on the gazebo's wooden bench, knees drawn up, chin resting on them.

They'd sneaked away while everyone was offering their best wishes to the couple. It was quieter here, the laughter and gaiety muted, as if the party were only a dream in the distance.

A soft breeze whispered through the sides of the gazebo, ruffling the ends of her hair, teasing the hem of her skirt. The moonlight shining through the latticework cast little squares of light over everything, dispelling the darkness of the night.

"We tried, we lost," Nick said in defeat, continuing to pace in front of her.

"We probably lost before we even began," Fiona pointed out, though it served no real purpose, except maybe to mitigate their sense of failure.

Nick didn't answer, only raked his hands through his hair. The moonlight illuminated the lines around his mouth, the worried creases in his forehead. He was more distressed than his philosophical remark had indicated.

Fiona wanted to soothe him, kiss away the creases of defeat in his face. "Maybe it'll be all right," she said. "Maybe everything will work out for them after all. I mean, what do we know? We could be worrying about nothing."

"Yeah—sure." His reply wasn't exactly overflowing with confidence.

She leaned back against the side of the gazebo, letting the full impact of the night wash over her. The wedding would take place the day after tomorrow, here, in this very spot. Her father would take Winnie as his new wife.

She squeezed her eyes shut and prayed he would find happiness, prayed Winnie wouldn't disappoint him the way Adam had disappointed her, that they loved each other enough to overlook each other's shortcomings, their idiosyncrasies, and be happy together.

Here Comes the Bride

She felt a stab of regret at the years her father and mother hadn't been able to share with each other, the happy carefree years after raising a family, struggling to build a life, to make ends meet.

Fiona felt the image of her mother slipping away and she didn't want it to. She wanted it to burn brightly forever. She wanted to hold on to it, to remember her mother as the center of their little family.

Nick glanced over at Fiona. Was it a trick of the moonlight or were there tears glazing her eyes? He'd been so wrapped up in his own concerns, he'd forgotten for a moment that Fiona was equally disappointed that the wedding was on again.

He remembered how she'd slipped her hand into his when Auntie and Walter had made their announcement. It had felt small and warm against his, both offering and asking for strength as they'd shared the moment together in the midst of the crowd of well-wishers.

She looked so small and delicate now, with her knees drawn up under her chin. The moonlight glistened over her hair, spinning each strand into creamy gold. He wanted to touch it, feel it spill between his fingers. He wanted to put his hand to her face, so pearl white in the soft light.

She was hurting and he wondered if a kiss would make her pain go away.

In the distance the party continued, the celebrating. He could hear the laughter. Someone had turned on a stereo and he could see a few couples dancing under the glow of the patio lights.

He moved toward Fiona and tilted her chin up to his gaze. Yes, there were tears there, soft, full ones. He brushed a finger under one lower lash. A warm droplet trickled onto his skin.

"May I have this dance, pretty lady?"

Her sweet mouth curved up into a faint smile, a tender counterpoint to the tears in her eyes. She uncurled her legs and stood, brushing down her skirt.

Her feet were bare. She'd taken off her sandals earlier and now left them on the bench where she'd been sitting, preferring to dance barefoot.

"I'll be careful not to step on your toes," he promised, leading her to the center of the gazebo.

Fiona slid into his arms, not the least worried about her toes, only her heart, which, minute by minute, she was losing to him. How had he known the only thing that could bring satisfaction to her soul at that moment, the light back into her life, was a dance? A quiet dance alone in the moonlight, the strains of the music thrumming on the night air. Something slow and seductive and dreamy.

She moved closer into his arms, fitting her head against his neck, and swayed to the rhythm, all thoughts temporarily forgotten save one: how wonderfully they meshed together, soft against hard, curve against plane. Two pieces made whole, like they'd been created just for each other.

She leaned into him, savoring the feel of him. He smelled like soap and shaving cream, and it was having a decided effect on her senses. She danced with both arms wound around his neck, her breasts pressed against the heat of him. Her fingers threaded through the silky hair at his nape as it curled over the collar of his shirt.

His breath was hot against her cheek, sending delicious little shivers along her spine. She wanted the dance to go on forever so she could spend forever in his arms.

Nick felt her snuggle in against him, her rounded breasts warm and full, a tempting delight that made him suck in a breath for control. What this woman's body could do to him was decadent. Sweet torture.

With one hand on her derriere he drew her tighter against him, fitting her into the cradle of his thighs. His other enjoyed the bare skin left exposed by her low-backed sundress, skin velvet-soft and smooth.

The intimacy of their position was nearly his undoing. He felt his body harden against her. She didn't draw away in response, but settled in more enticingly. He prayed she wouldn't squirm too much. Slow swaying to the music he could handle. But not much more.

"You're sweet," she said to him. "A sweet fake. You're not as hard-boiled as you'd like people to believe."

"Hard-boiled?" At the moment a part of him could fit the term.

"You asked me to dance with you when I was feeling at my lowest ebb, as if you could read me. Do you always know what a woman needs?"

Her words were torturing him, her voice a breathy whisper next to his ear. He wasn't sure he understood women at all, but he'd love to give this woman anything she wanted.

He'd love to read her body, intuitively sensing her every need, make love to her just to see her eyes shine with want, hear her voice ragged with passion. That would be his pleasure.

"I guess that's me, Mr. Romantic."

"Mmmm, you are that."

She wriggled against him and his breath caught as he nearly cried out in agony. She felt so good, he thought he'd die.

By the time the music stopped, he was

nearly crazy with wanting her. His head struggled to remind the rest of him that making love to Fiona would be a dangerous move, that she wasn't someone he could walk away from after a night of passion.

She was a woman who could make a man care—and a man hurt when the affair was over.

"Maybe we should get back before we're missed," he said, hating that it had to be this way.

"Mmmm."

She slid from his arms and Nick was sure he caught a look of wistful disappointment in her eyes. He swallowed hard and led her back to the sounds of celebrating.

Two cups of room-service coffee had Fiona's nerves jangled. Or maybe it was thoughts of last night, dancing with Nick alone in the gazebo. The memory of it haunted her, Nick's soft gaze, his touch—his tenderness. He'd seen the tears she hadn't wanted him to see, had brushed one gently away.

He'd known what she needed most at that moment. A dance. One simple dance in the moonlight. And it had turned her heart to mush.

Beneath that tough facade the man was

sensitive and caring, but few, she suspected, saw that side of Nick Killian.

Pacing to the window, she looked out. Another hot, sunny day in this desert town. The mountains shimmered a lovely purple in the distance, like a mirage. Several stories below her, cars made their way down the Strip. People moved along the sidewalks, trekking from hotel casino to hotel casino, day and night, night and day. The time didn't matter, only the lure of chance.

Fate. The town was built on fate, the whimsicalness of it, the cruelty of it. It caught everyone who ventured here. She'd thought herself immune. But was she?

Fate seemed to have a dangerous hold on her life right now. She was on the verge of falling head over heels in love with Nick and she didn't know what chance had in store for her.

A roll of the dice for high stakes in one of the gaming rooms downstairs seemed less of a risk.

Fiona turned from the window and checked her watch. It was eleven already. She'd whiled away the morning and she still had to shower and dress. She was meeting her father for lunch at a small restaurant near the hotel. She had decided to make one more stab at talking sense to her wayward parent.

What could it hurt?

Nick had had to fly to Los Angeles today to consult on a divorce case, so he wasn't around to have a heart-to-heart talk with Winnie.

Forty minutes later Fiona hurried through the casino toward the front entrance of the hotel, but a quarter slot machine winked and blinked at her as she passed by the last bank of them.

Why not? she thought. It was calling her name. She dug in her purse, finding three bright coins to feed the one-armed bandit.

The term *bandit* was apt, she decided as the thing ate up the first two quarters. She dropped in the third and pulled the handle again, cursing herself for the fool that she was.

Bells went off. Coins spilled out. Lots of them.

Feeling like a thief in the night, she scooped them up.

Maybe, just maybe, her luck was changing. Coins jingling in her purse and a song in her heart, she headed for the door.

Her father was waiting for her at the restaurant by the time she got there. She scooted into the chair across from him.

"I'm buying lunch," she told him, then turned her purse upside down on the table and spilled her winnings out.

He raked his fingers through the wealth.

"Well, Fiona, I think I'll just take you up on that, rich girl that you are."

They laughed like two children, something she hadn't done with him for a long while.

When the waiter arrived, they both ordered. Steak for her father and a giant salad for herself. "And bring us a carafe of your house wine, too," she added.

The waiter nodded, then glanced, not for the first time, at the pile of money on the table, no doubt hoping for a generous tip.

"I'm glad we have a chance to talk, Dad. We haven't had a minute to spend alone."

"I know. It's all this wedding folderol. Did you have a nice time last night, Fiona?"

Fiona studied his face for some hidden meaning, but it was an innocent question. He hadn't seen her slip away with Nick to the gazebo. Or the way Nick had held her when they'd danced, making her skin burn hot from his very touch.

"Yes, a nice time, Dad." A little too nice, she added silently. She hadn't been able to sleep last night for remembering it. She hadn't been able to get Nick out of her mind today. "I like Camille. We had a chance to talk, to get acquainted."

"Oh, that's good." He beamed. "I'd hoped we could all become a family."

A family. She didn't know about that.

Here Comes the Bride

What she felt for Nick was far from . . . cousinly.

Just then the waiter brought their order. When he disappeared again, Fiona took a slow sip of wine.

"So, Dad, I guess we'll have to find a home for your furniture, unless, of course, Winnie wants to mix it in with her things." She knew how he loved that old recliner of his—brown tweed, one broken leg, propped up with a copy of a Louis L'Amour novel.

His eyes widened at her across the table. "Furniture? We hadn't talked about my furniture."

"Well, I'm certain Winnie will work out something. The same way she'll find room for your collection of *National Geographic*, your baseball caps, the wine bottles, and your cuckoo clocks."

Unless her father had changed radically in the past few months, those clocks went off every hour, a raucous cacophony.

Walter Ames put down his steak knife with a clatter. "Fiona, what is it you're getting at?"

She set her wineglass on the table and leaned forward across her salad. "I'm asking if you're ready to give up your lifestyle for this woman?"

Her eyes bored into him, not allowing him to evade the issue. She wanted an answer.

"Lifestyle. That's one of those buzzwords

you young people throw around these days. Like relationship, involvement, feelings, verbal sharing. Claptrap, Fiona. Winnie and I love each other—bottom line."

"But, Dad, how do you know it's really love?"

"If it walks like a duck, quacks like a duck . . . Fiona, I don't have to examine it under a microscope. When it hits you, you know it's right."

His words bounced around in her head for a moment. *When it hits you.* She thought of Nick and that powerful force of something she felt whenever he smiled at her, touched her hand . . . kissed her.

But she barely knew Nick.

Her father didn't know Winnie.

Love did not happen overnight.

She'd been in love once, but time had proven that a mistake. And time could come along and crush her father, too.

She didn't want that for him. "Dad—"

"Fiona, I don't want to have any further discussion about where my furniture will or will not go. Winnie and I can work that out between us, I'm sure." His cheeks sported twin dots of high color. Hot indignation.

The man was stubborn. And adamant about his beloved Winnie. She wanted desperately to believe he was right, that everything would work out for them.

And maybe it would. She hoped so.

"Okay, Dad." She busied herself with her salad, chasing a cherry tomato around on her plate. As she gave her father a smile she inwardly resigned herself to tossing rice tomorrow night and toasting the happy twosome with champagne.

Fiona stood naked in front of the mirror in her small suite and checked for tan lines. She'd spent the afternoon soaking up the sun by one of the hotel's three Olympic-size swimming pools.

She'd felt as lazy as a beach bunny, but she hadn't cared. She was beginning to look like a native, a *rested* native. Her New England pallor had faded, replaced by a rich, golden tan. Not one dark circle hovered beneath her eyes. She turned, inspecting her backside.

The high cut of her swimsuit made her look like a leggy model and the bronzed color on her back dipped low enough to accommodate the immodest sundress she'd splurged on this afternoon in one of the pricey shops in her hotel.

She spun back around to face the front again, giving herself a frank appraisal. Her neck and shoulders had turned a glorious hue. She reached up and touched the smattering of freckles just above her breasts, tracing the irregular shape of one. Her breasts looked even paler against the contrast of color, high and rounded and pert, her nipples a dark, dusky pink.

She didn't exercise as regularly as she knew she should, but her body didn't seem to be lacking because of it. For a moment she wondered what Nick's assessment would be. Would he think she needed a workout on the Nautilus equipment? Or would he find her body tempting? Just right?

She'd been aware of his appreciative male gaze on her last night, and other times, a slow, thorough survey of her attributes. And when they'd danced alone in the gazebo, she'd felt the evidence of his arousal, had known that he'd wanted her.

And dammit, she'd wanted him.

More than she thought she could ever want any man. The intensity of it had made her tremble in his arms.

Then the music had stopped and the darkness crept into his eyes. He'd set his jaw firmly . . . and led her back to the party.

A slow sigh shuddered up from someplace deep inside her. Nick bore a pain in his soul that she didn't fully understand. And that she wasn't sure could be healed.

He'd be returning from L.A. tonight and would no doubt be at Winnie's for dinner, an invitation Fiona had neatly sidestepped. For two reasons. First, she'd hoped he'd have some private time with Winnie.

The second had to do with need, *her* need. She didn't know how she could sit across the table from Nick and make small talk when just his glance consumed her.

She gave in to another deep sigh, then crossed the room and slipped naked between the sheets for a late-afternoon nap. Maybe later she'd order up room service and make her evening as decadently lazy as this afternoon had been.

Fiona awoke to the intrusive sound of the phone ringing. She thought she'd been asleep only a short while, but the room was dark. Hours must have passed. The faint red glow of the alarm clock's dial showed it was late, indeed. Nine thirty-five.

A faint wisp of a dream still lingered in the darker recesses of her mind. A dream about Nick—slightly erotic and so real she was bathed in a sheen of sweat.

At the continued insistent jangle she reached for the phone, trying to clear the cobwebs of sleep and the fading dream from her head.

"Hello." Her voice sounded froggy and deep, like it belonged to someone else.

"Fiona?"

Nick wasn't sure it was Fiona. She sounded different. Her voice low and sexy with sleep. It made him want her so badly he ached from the need. He'd missed her all day, had thought of her at moments when his mind should have been on other things.

He remembered her scent last night in the gazebo, the fragrance of her hair when they'd danced, clean and fresh, like a bouquet of newly picked flowers that still carried the scent of the sun.

"Oh, Nick, hi." Fiona sat up in bed, trying to orient herself. The sheet fell to her waist and she remembered her nakedness. The hotel's air-conditioning had chilled the room and she raised the sheet to her shoulders.

"Had you gone to bed already? I didn't mean to wake you."

She dragged a hand through the tumble of her hair. "You didn't . . . I mean, that's okay. I'd just taken an afternoon nap."

"Fiona, it's not afternoon." Nick wondered what she slept in, a funny little nightshirt or . . . nothing. He groaned. Either way the image was too tantalizing to deal with right now. He needed to know if Fiona was all right. "Are you okay? I mean, you're not ill or anything?"

"No, I'm not ill."

He heard her shift, heard the faint rustle of sheets, and for one crazy moment found himself jealous of those sheets that touched her body.

He sighed and tried to get a grip. "We missed you at Auntie's." *He* missed her at Auntie's. Very much. Had expected to see her there. And when he didn't, when Walter said she wasn't coming, disappointment, all-pervasive and swift, settled over him.

Not a good omen, not for a man who believed he didn't need a woman, one special woman, in his life. He could only hope it was a need that would pass.

"I'm sorry," she said. "I hope Winnie's not offended, but I just needed some time alone."

"Alone?" He didn't like to think of her being alone. Or more honestly, he didn't like to think that Fiona preferred being alone to being with him. That she didn't need to see him as much as he needed to see her.

"I could come over," he said, then cursed himself for the words. If he got within ten feet of her, saw her looking soft and inviting and warm, he'd want to make love to her. "I mean, what are you going to do about dinner?"

"I'd planned to order up something from room service."

"Oh." For the second time that night he tasted swift disappointment. He really had to get a grip.

"Nick . . ."

"Yes?" His answer was too quick, telltale quick. He hoped she was going to say that she'd changed her mind, that she wanted to see him.

He realized he was holding his breath. Like some adolescent schoolboy who'd asked the prettiest girl in class to the prom and was praying she'd smile at him and say she'd go.

Never before had a woman had this kind of hold on him.

"I was going to say . . ."

She had him on tenterhooks.

"I was going to say I had a talk with my father today and—"

"A talk with Walter?"

"Yes."

It was back to business, the business of their wayward relatives. Was that what had occupied the better part of her thoughts today? The wedding? Not him? Not what was happening between them?

"And how did it go? The talk with your father?"

"Nick, he says they're in love, that—"

Fiona heard Nick's derisive snort on the other end of the line. He clearly didn't believe for a moment that they were in love. After spending the day consulting on another divorce case, his cynicism would be running high.

Maybe he had a right to be cynical. Marriage was a risky proposition these days and Nick was in a position to know that. "My father seems so sure everything will work out."

"Yeah, well, I'm not so sure."

Fiona didn't know how she felt anymore. All she knew was that just the sound of Nick's voice as it purled over the phone line made her heart thump faster, made her wish he was here so she could see him . . . touch him.

Then she remembered her resolve, the reason she'd stayed away from dinner at Winnie's. She needed to keep her distance from Nick.

Before she did something foolish like fall in love with him. A man who didn't believe in love.

"I'm just a little down after my day," he said. "Sorry. I didn't mean to inflict that on you. I know you're worried."

"You didn't inflict anything on me, Nick. I understand how you feel."

Neither of them spoke for a moment.

Fiona didn't want the conversation to end. She wanted to hear his voice, its velvet timbre that did such dangerous things to her senses.

She fluffed the pillow at her back and leaned against its softness, drinking in the knowledge that Nick was there. Close—yet a safe distance away.

"I don't know if it'll do any good or not,

but I'll have a talk with Auntie," he said finally.

"Thanks, Nick."

Nick didn't want to end the conversation, didn't want to let Fiona go, but there was nothing else to say. He didn't understand what it was that was happening to him with this woman, but he knew he was playing with fire.

"I . . . I'd better go. I'll call you in the morning and let you know if I had any luck with Auntie."

EIGHT

Nick did not call the next morning. Instead he showed up. Fiona opened the door to her hotel room to find him standing there in the hallway, looking tall, dark, gorgeous . . .

And worried.

Her eyes widened in surprise and her breath caught in her throat, both at the sight of him and at the concerned expression on his face.

"It's Auntie," he said. "She fell off a stepladder while she and Camille were decorating the gazebo. Your father just called me from the hospital."

"Oh, Nick."

"I don't know how badly she's hurt. I just told Walter I'd come get you; we'd be right there."

Fiona swept back her hair with one hand.

She didn't have time to run a brush through its thickness or even change clothes from the pink shorts and Las Vegas T-shirt she'd slipped on after her shower. From the look of Nick, he was eager for them to get on their way.

He was clearly worried about his aunt, and Fiona was worried about her father. If Winnie was seriously hurt, her father would be a wreck.

Fiona remembered when she was ten years old and had fallen out of a tree and broken her collarbone. Her father hadn't left her side. Instead he'd paced beside the gurney they'd placed her on in the emergency room, ordering the doctors to do something and generally getting in the way.

"I'll just grab my purse," she told Nick. She snatched it off the bed, checked to see if she had her room key, and followed Nick out the door.

After an endlessly slow elevator ride they reached the lobby. Nick was three paces ahead of her across its expanse. He looked like he'd been dressed for the office, though he'd shed his suit jacket and tie somewhere along the way and turned back the sleeves of his soft blue shirt. His hair was tousled, either from the desert breeze or from raking his hands through it. She didn't know which.

"Is the hospital far?" she asked when they'd reached the hotel entrance.

Nick shook his head and held the door for her. "Not more than ten blocks."

Nick had left the Porsche in a no-parking zone when he'd raced inside to get Fiona. He tipped the doorman ten bucks for not having the car towed. When he turned back, Fiona was sliding into the passenger seat. Her pink shorts rode up a delectable few inches on her tanned legs, a view he wished he had more time to enjoy. Swallowing a groan, he rounded the car and slipped in behind the wheel.

"I told Auntie to wait until Walter and I could string those damned wedding garlands for her," he said, pulling out into traffic. "But she wouldn't listen."

If Winnie was stringing wedding flowers in the gazebo this morning, she hadn't listened to Nick's little talk last night, Fiona surmised.

She didn't even need to ask how the conversation had gone. She knew it chapter and verse. She was certain it was the same she'd gotten from her father. The couple knew their own minds. And a few well-pointed objections from Fiona and Nick weren't about to change it.

Within minutes Nick pulled into the crowded visitors' parking lot, then grasped her hand as they hurried toward the ER entrance. Inside, they spotted Camille. She sat on the edge of a waiting-room chair, nervously thumbing the glossy pages of a magazine that she didn't look like she was reading. She jumped up as they entered.

"Is she okay?" Nick asked. "Did she break anything?"

"They're waiting for the X-ray reports now. It's her ankle. This is all my fault," Camille said. "I shouldn't have let her climb on that stepladder to hang those silly flowers."

"Don't blame yourself, Camille," Fiona told her. "Is my father with her?"

"Yes. They would only allow one person in there. Have a seat. Walter's been giving me progress reports."

Nick paced the length of the waiting room. Fiona joined Camille on a chair and listened as Camille explained how the unfortunate accident had occurred and how the headstrong Winnie never listened to reason.

The pair—her father and Winnie—were well matched on that score at least, Fiona thought. Headstrong and stubborn to a fault.

A short while later Walter stepped into the waiting area. He looked a little pale and his sandy-gray hair was mussed, no doubt from nervous fingers, but he was smiling.

Nick approached and grasped his arm. "Is Auntie okay? What did the doctor say? Is he a good one?" He didn't want Winnie treated by some snot-nosed intern no older than Doogie Howser.

"Her ankle isn't broken," Walter reported. "It's just a bad sprain. At the moment Winnie's giving the doctor what-for about the thick wrap he's putting on to immobilize it."

Nick studied his face to be certain that this was the whole truth, that Walter wasn't holding anything back. Auntie wasn't married *yet*. Nick was still responsible for her welfare.

Just then the ER doors slid open and Winnie hobbled through, leaning inexpertly on a pair of crutches. Her right foot was encased in the cumbersome-looking wrap.

Nick hurried to her side at the same moment Walter did. She listed to the left, accepting Walter's strengthening arm—not Nick's.

Nick took a step back, relinquishing his hold. He'd always been there for her—and now she didn't want his help, just Walter's.

"Good gracious," Winnie muttered. "You didn't all have to come down here."

"We were worried about you, Mother," Camille said.

"Worried? It's nothing but a silly sprain. I tried to tell that nervous Nellie of a doctor just that, but he trussed me up like a partridge and told me I had to use these cursed crutches.

I'm telling you I'll really break something trying to get used to them."

"Now, Winnie dearest, it's for your own good," Walter soothed. "Let's get you home, then Nick and I will finish stringing those flowers for the wedding."

"The wedding?" Winnie's brows all but descended to the bridge of her nose and her eyes narrowed. She looked askance at her trussed-up leg. "There isn't going to be any wedding. Not tonight. I'm not about to march down the aisle to my intended looking like this," she said, then hobbled her way toward the exit, Walter in tow.

Fiona and Camille spent the afternoon calling all the wedding guests, explaining that the ceremony was off until some future date and accepting regrets about Winnie's infirmity. These they passed on to the patient, who lounged nearby on a blue-green chaise in the family room, alternately fuming over her ruined wedding and enjoying her future husband's loving ministrations.

Walter catered to her every whim, plumping her pillow, bringing her fresh-made lemonade, and settling tiny kisses on her brightly painted toes, which peeped out from the thick elastic wrap.

Finally the last guest had been contacted.

So had the minister, the caterer, and sundry others who were to have performed services connected to the night's festivities.

Fiona breathed a sigh of relief, excused herself from the group, and headed for the kitchen for a tall glass of lemonade like the one Winnie was enjoying. Nick glanced up from the crossword puzzle he'd been frowning over at the breakfast bar.

"What's a six-letter word for *interloper*?" he asked. "W-a-l-t-e-r doesn't fit."

Fiona finished pouring her drink, then set the pitcher down with a thunk. "What's that supposed to mean?"

Nick scowled. "Your father's been hovering over Auntie all afternoon, pampering her silly."

"And you feel unneeded," she added for him. She knew how much he loved his aunt, saw how worried he'd been about her. Since his uncle Gray died, he'd been the one to look after her, care for her—now Fiona's father was doing that. And Nick didn't like it. Nick didn't trust him, any man, to make her happy.

"They haven't even noticed the rest of us are around."

"I think that's called love," Fiona said, realizing the pair were indeed very much in love.

He gave a disapproving snort. He didn't believe in love, any more than he believed in marriage. But she was having second thoughts about her father's relationship with Winnie.

Fiona had always thought love needed to be developed, nurtured, allowed to bloom. She didn't believe love could spring to life so quickly between two people, but it obviously had for her father and Winnie.

She'd seen it shining brightly in his eyes as he catered to Winnie's every need. She saw it in Winnie's eyes as she allowed his solicitous pampering.

"So, did you get all the calls made? Is the wedding officially off again?"

"The wedding's officially off."

For how long, Fiona didn't know. She didn't know whether to stay here in town until it was on again or go home to Boston.

Each day she stayed she knew she was at risk, at risk of falling in love with Nick. Falling in love as quickly as her father had with Winnie.

She sighed and leaned back against the bright tiled countertop. Maybe it was something in the water here. Maybe it was the hot desert wind, firing up passions. She didn't know. All she knew was that she was deep in danger.

"Since we're not needed here, wanna blow this joint?" Nick asked. He shoved aside the unfinished crossword puzzle and came over to nuzzle her neck.

"Leave?"

"Yes, leave."

His breath whispered down the neckline of her T-shirt, sending dangerous little shivers skittering over her body. She tried to ignore it . . . *him* . . . and took a sip of lemonade. Between its delicious coolness and Nick's nuzzling nips to her delicate skin, she was transported. Heat curled low inside her.

She longed to slide into his embrace and spend the rest of the day and all of the night there, being loved and wooed by him. But did she dare? Nick was a man who could shred her heart.

"Kiss me, Fiona." His voice was a soft command, an order from some baser part of him. It reached out to some baser part of herself, one she couldn't ignore. Like someone drugged into willingness, she sought the urgency of his lips.

"Mmmm, you taste like lemonade," he murmured. He drew his tongue with infinite slowness over her top lip, then her lower, rasping every nerve ending into life. He nipped; he kissed; he stroked; he caressed. Until Fiona was quivering.

He reached for her glass that she'd barely touched and set it down on the counter behind her. "I want both your hands free to roam over me," he said with that naughty smile she knew not to trust.

Widening his stance, he straddled her frame, pinning her against the countertop, against him, like a prisoner without a will. The heat of his arousal pressed into her and she sucked in a breath, barely able to control her own need.

Nick was all-encompassing whenever he was around—and even when he wasn't. He filled her thoughts, he filled her dreams. She wanted to touch him, every inch of him. No, not touch, but stroke, explore, caress, drink in his maleness with her fingertips.

She could feel the hard plane of muscle beneath his shirt as she ran the palms of her hands over his chest. His own traveled down her back, making her spinal column as limp as a noodle. All the while his mouth teased and tortured and plundered hers, sapping her of strength.

She hoped no one came into the kitchen, hoped this feeling could go on forever, this feeling of being owned by Nick. The feeling that she possessed him as well. For she knew she did, if only for this moment.

She moved her hands over the wide expanse of his shoulders, where his sinewy muscles bunched and relaxed beneath her touch. She brushed her fingers up the strong column of his neck, feeling his pulse throb there, sure and powerful, in sync with her own thudding heartbeat. Her fingertips learned the shape of his jaw, the curve of his ear. She wanted, needed, to know the feel of him.

"You're setting me on fire, woman," Nick groaned as he reveled in her tentative explorations. He wanted to peel off his clothes, let her touch him everywhere. He wanted to strip her naked and return the pleasure tenfold.

"That's not the half of what you do to me, Nick Killian." Her soft voice was a seductive whisper next to his ear, as if the words came from some secret place deep inside her.

"Have dinner with me tonight, Fiona. Just us. Away from the family." His request was a plea, one he hoped she wouldn't refuse.

"I . . . I don't know if that's a good idea, Nick."

"I make a mean omelette. Now, how can you refuse a free meal from such a charming guy?"

He tilted her chin up. A small worried frown had insinuated itself between her pretty eyebrows. She was afraid. Of him? Of what was happening between them?

Oh, Lord, so was he. Terrified. He couldn't remember a woman who'd had this kind of hold on him. And he didn't want it to end. Not yet.

Her green-eyed gaze swept his face, as if searching for reassurance that her heart . . . and her virtue . . . would be safe with him.

He prayed his eyes didn't reflect a hint of

the lust he felt in his soul at that moment and swore to himself this would be an innocent little dinner between them. Above all else he wanted her company.

When her answer came, it was soft and whispery. "Okay, Nick."

His heart soared.

Before she had a chance to change her mind, he swept her through the family room, uttered hasty good-byes to the rest of the family, and spirited her away to his car.

The man was gorgeous and he cooked, too. A woman would be lucky to land him.

Fiona sat on a bar stool in Nick's state-of-the-art kitchen, holding a goblet of rosé wine, and pondered what sort of woman might fit into his life. Someone tall, chic, and sophisticated came to mind.

Try as she might, the title *wife* didn't seem to work. A live-in would be more to his liking. A woman who came with no strings and who wanted none herself.

He propped open the door of the fridge with one lean hip as he sorted through ingredients for their omelettes. "Monterey Jack, green peppers, fresh mushrooms," he enumerated, placing each item on the red-tiled countertop beside him.

"I vote for all of the above," she answered.

Here Comes the Bride

Fiona enjoyed his deft movements, the way his off-white slacks fit his sexy, male tush, the way the fine linen of his shirt hugged his muscled torso. She knew what those muscles felt like beneath the fabric of that shirt. She'd memorized them with her fingertips a short while before—and she liked what she'd found. Nick Killian was solid male. She'd felt his vibrancy and his heat.

And it excited her.

"So, do you cook often?" she asked, deciding to keep her mind on dinner instead of what came with the meal—Nick.

He turned and smiled at her. "Define what you mean by often."

To her, more than once a month would be often. She had very little time for the culinary arts, beyond a fast sandwich or a salad hurriedly tossed together before she had to get back to the business of running her shop. "Do you entertain?"

One dark eyebrow rose in amusement. "Ah, the lady has a nosy streak."

"Dinner parties," she added quickly. "Do you do dinner parties?"

He shook his head. "I'm not into the social scene, if that's what you mean. I prefer to keep things simple. A few healthy meals for myself, an occasional barbecue, that sort of thing."

He took out a butcher-block chopping board and began dicing ingredients.

"If you don't think too many cooks spoil the broth, I can help," she offered, setting down her wineglass.

He turned and smiled. "How are you at beating eggs?"

"Just try me."

His smile widened. "Don't tempt me, lady."

She felt a hot blush taint her cheeks. "I meant my ability."

His eyebrow only raised.

"My *egg-beating* ability," she clarified.

He shoved a bowl and whisk toward her. "Let's see some wrist action then," he said in challenge.

She slid off the bar stool and reached for a blue apron, dangling from the copper peg rack on the wall, carefully avoiding the red one with the invitation to kiss the cook. She suspected the man didn't need any encouragement. There was danger enough just being in this kitchen with him. "Wrist action coming up."

She cracked eggs while he grated cheese, working side by side. It was a nice feeling—like when they'd spent the day exploring the ghost town.

Fiona beat the eggs harder. She was beginning to forget she had another life, a life to go back to once this wedding finally came off, a whole other existence, one that didn't include a man with beautiful shoulders and a powder-blue shirt that rendered his eyes more vivid than the sky.

Nick's broad hand came down on hers. "Don't beat 'em to death, Fiona. Use a gentle touch so you don't break down the protein."

She glanced up. "Right. Gentle."

A short while later they were seated on the floor of the living room, Nick's perfect omelettes spread out on the glass-topped coffee table in front of them.

"Nick, this is wonderful," she said after one bite, a bite that had melted in her mouth. The man could definitely cook.

"We make a good team," he said with a dangerous smile. He leaned over and refilled her wineglass.

The wine, the food, the evening alone with Nick was a heady experience. She wanted him to kiss her again. Like he had earlier in Winnie's kitchen. Once or twice she'd thought he might when his gaze had strayed to her mouth, lingering there just long enough to raise her body temperature.

Or maybe it was the wine. It was a light blend, with a delicate bouquet, that went well with the fluffy omelettes. She took another sip and studied him over her goblet. He ate with gusto. It was, no doubt, the way he did everything. . . .

That thought made her smile. Nick would

be the perfect lover, hot, passionate, giving. She set her goblet down on the coffee table, realizing she'd had far too much.

"So, you think your father and Auntie are in love." Nick didn't look at her, but concentrated on his plate. "When did this change of heart occur, might I ask?"

She tucked her feet under her on the floor. She'd kicked off her sandals earlier, making herself comfortable in his living room. "Today," she said quietly. "Watching them together, seeing the concern in my father's eyes, the brightness in Winnie's. Nick, I've decided to take back my objections to this wedding. If it's what Dad wants, what Winnie wants, then I intend to be happy for them."

Nick glanced over at Fiona, studying her for a long moment. She meant it. She was selling out, going over to the other side, leaving him as the only dissenting voice. "I see."

"Nick, I'm sorry, but it's how I feel. The only thing I've ever wanted was for my father to be happy—and I think he can be, *will* be, with Winnie."

He took a swallow of wine. "Then you believe two very different people can be happy together?"

"In certain circumstances, yes. At least, that seems to be the case with Dad and Winnie."

He pushed a straying tendril of hair away

Here Comes the Bride

from her face, his fingers brushing her cheek. Her hair was soft and thick and he wanted to plunge his hands into it, revel in its luxuriousness. "And what about us, Fiona? We're just as different."

She started to speak, then stopped and caught her lower lip with her even white teeth, worrying it slightly. At that moment he knew he wanted to kiss her, *had* to kiss her, to taste the differences between them.

He inclined his head, lowering his mouth to hers, to the sweetness he knew he'd find there. He found that and more. He found need, need as strong as his own; and that, he feared, would be his undoing.

He wished one of them had the power to say no, to pull away, to end this now. He wished one of them had the power to resist the temptation that had hung in the air between them, possibly from the first moment they'd met, certainly from the first moment they'd kissed.

As he sank into the divine taste of her, he knew the power to resist wouldn't come from him. He didn't possess it.

They didn't touch—except for their lips—but he felt as hot as if Fiona had her hands on him. He kissed each succulent corner of her mouth, then the sensitive skin along her neck. "Different is nice," she murmured. "Very nice."

He was dying here—drowning in the scent of her, the flowery fragrance of her hair, her musky feminine scent of want, need.

He had to touch her, had to feel her softness, her heat. Hand trembling, he slid his wineglass onto the coffee table, then cupped her face between his palms. With his thumbs he stroked the hot blush of her cheeks, while his mouth sought hers again. He could romance those lips all night, until she was swollen from the taste of him. He kissed them, bathed them with his tongue, nipped their fullness.

She made a soft groan of pleasure and murmured his name. Her voice, low and husky, vibrated on his senses. His name had never sounded so intimate as it did falling from her lips.

He drew her against him. This time it was his turn to groan out in pleasure as she wound her arms around his neck and pressed her lush breasts into him. Yes, different was very nice, indeed.

He reveled in the differences of man and woman, this one woman, who fit so perfectly against him. He groaned again as he thought about their other parts that would fit together so perfectly, too.

Fiona was certain nothing would ever feel so right as this, the taste of Nick's mouth on hers, their bodies pressed against each other—

his, hard and strong and male, and hers, soft and pliant and female.

She could sense the barely controlled passion in him and knew that she held the power to unleash it, to tempt him into dangerous territory, territory from which there would be no going back. It was a power that carried with it a frisson of fear as well as a headiness. And it was that headiness she relished at that moment.

His tongue teased at her lips, begging them to part. "Open for me, Fiona." His words were a warm murmur, a command, and a supplication.

She possessed no will to refuse him. Her lips parted, quivering with her need for him. He tasted like the wine they'd shared and the saltiness of their evening feast. He sampled and explored as if to learn all her moist secrets. Heat coiled through her, spreading like a river of wildfire along her veins, then coalesced in a blaze at the core of her being.

She wanted Nick Killian, wanted him to make love to her. Now. Tonight. It was a decision born of passion, not reason. She'd lost all sense of reason with that first kiss. She knew she'd regret this tomorrow, but tomorrow was a long time away.

"Make love to me, Nick." Fiona barely recognized her own voice. It was ragged with unspent passion, husky with want.

Nick sucked in a breath, Fiona's request sobering him. He drew back and framed her face with his hands. He wanted her, wanted her now, more than he'd ever wanted any woman. But a sense of right warred with opportunity. This was Fiona asking, a woman who could possess his soul, a woman who believed in happily-ever-afters and lifetime commitments.

And although the thought of making love to her for a lifetime held delicious possibilities, he knew nothing, least of all commitments, lasted forever.

Fiona stared into his face that was full of doubt—and something else, something indefinable. She'd blundered. Nick was a man who wanted to make all the moves. He'd been turned off by her blatant proposal of lovemaking.

Or maybe she'd misread him. Maybe he wanted only a bit of innocent fooling around, not to share his bed with her.

She felt like a fool and her cheeks flamed beneath his hands. She grasped his wrists, ready to break the only physical connection they shared, except for his stunned gaze that hadn't left her face. "Nick, forget that, forget I asked—"

"I don't think I can forget, Fiona." If he lived to be a thousand, he'd never forget the seductive sweetness of that asking. He'd never had a proposition more enticing.

"Try," she begged.

She dragged his hands from her face, then turned away from him, but not before Nick had seen the heat in her cheeks. She'd misunderstood his hesitation, thought he didn't want her when, God help him, the exact reverse was true. He wanted her so badly, his body sang with an ache so keen, so exquisite, he was certain a night of cold showers couldn't soothe it.

"Fiona, look at me. . . ."

"I—I can't."

He reached for her chin and stroked it with the flat of his thumb. Just touching her made his body throb with an agonized ache. "I want you," he said, his throat nearly closing off with desire.

She shook her head. "Don't go all chivalrous on me, Nick. The lady asked, so the lady should be obliged—I don't need that."

"I know what you need and it's the same thing I need." He drew her hand to his body, placing it against his hardened flesh. "Does that feel like chivalry?"

He prayed for control. The feel of her warmth against him nearly sent him into orbit. He struggled for clarity. Truth. Fiona needed the truth. "I only hesitated because I know I can't give you what you want, Fiona."

She withdrew her hand and turned her face up to his. It was beautiful in the dim glow from the lamp. So perfect, so trusting.

"I can't give you forever, not because I don't want to . . ." He wanted to reach into the night sky and pluck down the moon for her. And half a dozen stars to go with it. ". . . but because I don't believe in forevers."

Tears welled in her eyes. "Oh, Nick, I know that, and I wasn't asking for forever. I wasn't thinking past this night, this moment."

"*I* was. I didn't want you to be hurt."

Nick couldn't hurt her; Fiona could only do that to herself. If she let him stroke her cheek the way he was doing now, if she let him caress her with his soft gaze, if she didn't pick up and run from his condo this very minute.

"I should send you away for your own good," he whispered, "but heaven help me, I don't think I can."

"Oh, Nick."

He didn't say another word, just reached out and kissed her, long and deep and hungrily. Then he picked her up and carried her to his bed.

NINE

Nothing about the room registered in Fiona's mind, except maybe the moonlight that streamed through the windows, painting them in a cool, silver glow.

Nick set her on her feet in the center of the bedroom and kissed her again, slowly, tenderly. Then he drew back and studied her for a quiet moment. She knew he was offering her the space to think, to change her mind about what they were on the brink of.

She tried to summon up her good sense, but the man standing there in front of her eclipsed it. There was not a shred left to taunt her into flight, retreat.

She wasn't thinking about forever; she wasn't even thinking about tomorrow. She reached up and traced his lips with the tip of one finger and was sure she heard him swallow hard, a reaction to her touch. It made her feel wanton.

She lowered her hands to the first closed button on his shirt and slowly, methodically, worked it loose, then the next. Whenever her fingers brushed against his bare flesh, his body tautened, further proof that she affected him.

Her courage, her blatancy climbed the Richter scale.

His hands rested on her shoulders and he slowly kneaded them as she worked. When she came to the last button above his belt, she tucked her fingers beneath it to free the tail of his shirt. His abdomen went washboard hard and he sucked in a breath.

A laugh rose up from her throat.

"You think this is funny?" he asked. "Just wait until I get to you."

Delicious heat suffused her.

She undid the final button and parted the fabric, then ran her palms across his chest, over the muscles beneath his hot skin, tangling her fingers in the dark chest hair.

Leaning close, she sucked one flat nipple. At his groan of approval she moved to the other, planting a kiss on it, then laving it with her tongue. He grew rigid, holding himself in taut control. Heady with excitement, she trailed one nail down the center of his chest to his belt and struggled to work the buckle. She was suddenly shaky, all thumbs.

"I could offer the lady a little assistance, but I think I'm enjoying this."

Oh, he was enjoying this, Fiona was sure of that. She could tell by the way he tensed as he tried to restrain himself, his soft gasp of pleasure at her touch. Nick was hers, all hers, at least for tonight.

Finally she got the buckle loose and reached for the zipper below it, lowering it over his hardness, the proof he wanted her. She let her fingers brush against his firm erection as she eased the metal lower. He sucked in a breath and grasped her hand. "You're killing me, Fiona. Driving me mad. But then I think you know that."

She suppressed a laugh. "I know that."

"Well, just remember, paybacks are hell."

Oh, it wouldn't be hell; it would be heaven and then some, Fiona was sure, but she let him finish the task of getting out of his slacks. He did so in haste, discarding his shoes and socks.

Fiona gasped as he stood there before her in the moonlight, clad only in taut, straining briefs and his unbuttoned dress shirt, like some magnificent warrior, male and fierce. She smiled at his underwear—a passion-red body-molding silk. "These aren't as wild as the tiger stripes that tumbled out of your suitcase that day at the airport," she said in a soft whisper.

"Fiona, about that underwear. I have to confess, lady-killer briefs are not my usual style. They were a prize at a bachelor auction. One female official's idea of an . . . honorarium for participating."

Fiona wasn't sure whether she could believe that or not. But whatever the story, he was wearing them now, looking enticingly male and lusty.

She swallowed hard. He was beautiful, tanned and lean, shoulders wide, hips narrow, legs strong and powerful, and she looked her fill. Then he tilted her chin up and tasted her lips, a slow, heated kiss, full of the promise of what was to come. "I want to see you naked, Fiona," he murmured against her mouth, his breath caressing and hot.

She shivered slightly. Her boldness of a few moments before dissipated. She stood stock-still as he ran his fingertips over her skin, the curve of her neck, the length of her arms. He found the hem of her T-shirt and teased the garment up and over her head, then dropped it to the floor beside them. His gaze skimmed her lacy white bra, then he bent and planted a kiss on the rounded swell of each breast that peeked above the cup.

Heat coiled through her and she tangled her fingers in his hair as he slipped his tongue beneath the fabric, bathing the delicate skin there. Fiona arched against him, wanting more.

"Help me get you out of this," he murmured, reaching for her back clasp.

She loved his clumsiness with women's apparel, despite the fact that she suspected he'd had plenty of experience ridding women of their intimate clothing. But she didn't want to think of that now. She reached back and undid the closure.

Nick's breath caught at the sight of her. With her hands still half behind her back, the lacy scrap of her bra slid away, revealing her high, firm breasts and her nipples, taut and dusky pink in the moonlight.

He caught her arms, pinning them there behind her back as he flicked his tongue first over one, then the other raised nub. He heard her sharp gasp as he slowly circled each.

It was only fair that she endure a little of the sweet misery she'd inflicted on him. He wanted to bring her pleasure, more than she could stand. He wanted to hear her cry out his name and arch against him, unable to bear the passion. He wanted her to belong to him tonight, solely and completely.

He kissed his way downward along her breastbone, over her flat, firm stomach. Then, reaching the waist of her pink shorts, he slipped them down the length of her, letting them pool at her feet. He ran his hands over the pink lace of her panties, feeling her heated skin through the fabric. He'd wanted to make love to her slowly, make it last for both of them, but he wasn't sure he could hold out much longer. He hooked his thumbs in the elastic band and shimmied the scrap off her.

Something mystical came over him when he saw her standing there nude before him. In the cool glow of the moonlight, she could have been a flawless alabaster statue—except that he'd felt the fire and fever of her. Fiona wasn't stone. She was all-too-real flesh and blood. And in a short while she'd be all his.

He trailed a finger over her hipbone. "Oh, lady, you are so beautiful."

Fiona trembled beneath Nick's touch. He caught her hand in his, then led her to the edge of the bed. There, he paused.

"I want to make love to you, Fiona, but only if you're sure you want this."

She knew that if she hesitated with even a flicker of an eyelid, he'd wrap her in her clothes and send her on her way. And that she couldn't bear.

"I want you, too, Nick. And I'm very sure."

He picked her up then and placed her in the center of the bed. For a moment he only gazed down at her, stretched out on the sheets. She wondered what he was thinking. That she looked so right there in his bed?

That he wanted her there always? Or did niggling doubt tease at him? "Nick . . ."

He didn't allow her to finish—for fear she'd changed her mind. He slid out of his briefs, the moonlight slanting across him making him look all the more ready in his total nakedness, more fierce than a moment before.

Her mouth went dry as he joined her on the bed. She loved the feel of him against her, hard and totally male. She went all moist with want of him.

His hands, so slow, so sure, spread out over her. His mouth found hers in a claiming kiss, his tongue thrusting and plunging in a sensual rhythm. Desire welled in her, sending her emotions whirling, and she reached for him. He was hot and needy and powerful.

His lips left hers and journeyed over her fevered skin, kissing, nipping. He found one nipple and suckled it. Her body peaked with rising need. With equal measure he sampled the other, teasing, tempting. His hand found the moistness between her legs and his fingers slid inside. She shuddered against his touch.

"Oh, Nick, you're driving me crazy."

"I want you beyond crazy, sweet lady. I want you in ecstasy."

Nick was nearly there himself. With her exquisite hold on him, he was about to explode. He willed himself to hold on, hold on until she was more than ready for him.

His mouth tasted her skin, trailing hot little kisses down to her navel, dipping into the sweetness there, then continued the journey along the silky length of her leg, the sensitive arch of her foot, her ticklish toes. His return trip took in the other leg, back up to her thigh, to the moist heat of her. He kissed her there, finding her ready. His tongue flickered over the core of her femininity until she writhed beneath him and begged for surfeit.

"Now, Nick," she ordered in the sexiest, most determined voice he thought he'd ever heard.

Nick knew he had to protect her. He searched the drawer of the table beside the bed and found the blue foil he was seeking. "Hold on, sweet love."

He hated the moment of interruption, but he couldn't hurt Fiona. With fumbling hands he slipped on the protection, then poised over her, he slid into the glorious heaven of her. He waited until she'd adjusted to him, then began to move inside her in the rhythm of the ages.

He watched her face in the soft moonlight, wanting this to be good for her. Her cheeks were flushed with passion and her hair spilled across the pillow. He buried his hands in its silk as she tightened her legs around him. Soon he was lost in abandon.

Fiona's body suffused with heat, the fire of

passion, as she climbed with Nick to unexplored heights. Sweat beaded his face, glistening in the moonlight that slanted over them.

This felt so right, so perfect. Her breath matched his until she thought her lungs would burst. Then she found release. It shuddered through her like waves crashing against a shoreline, never-ending. She murmured Nick's name, called it out from somewhere deep inside her, just as Nick shuddered with the same release.

He stayed there, holding her long afterward, caressing the damp tendrils of her hair away from her fevered face. Slowly her breath returned, her heartbeat slowed, and satisfaction, complete and thorough, ebbed through her.

Nick kissed each eyelid that had shuttered closed with languor, then the tip of her nose. An audible purr slid from her lips and he kissed those, too, not an awakening kiss, but one of satisfied passion.

They held each other for long moments, whispering intimacies. Fiona didn't know she could feel so replete, so filled, so cherished. She curled into the heat of him, not wanting to lose this newfound closeness. She knew she had, without any doubt, fallen in love with this man—a man who scoffed at love, at marriage. But she didn't want to dwell on that. She only wrapped her arms tighter around him. At least for tonight he'd shown her he was very capable of the love part.

They awoke several times throughout the night and found each other, making love again—quick and passionate love, slow and lazy love. Both kinds were wonderful, binding her to Nick even more, sealing her love for him.

The last time she awoke, the moonlight had faded. Sunlight flooded the room. She glanced at Nick, sleeping soundly beside her. His dark lashes fanned across his cheeks and his eyelids flickered slightly as if he was dreaming.

What were those dreams about? she wondered. Her? What they'd shared last night? A shiver of excitement danced through her and she wanted him again.

She wanted him in the daylight so she could watch what he did to her body with such mastery. She leaned close and brushed his lips with hers. They twitched in his sleep, then curved into a slight smile, but he didn't awaken.

With a sigh she glanced around the room, the room she'd taken little notice of last night. His bedroom was large and airy, the furniture a rich, tasteful cherrywood. The bed was big and soft—and wonderful for making love.

In their passion they'd tangled the sheets

hopelessly. Only one corner of the dark blue stripe kept Nick decent, barely covering his lower torso.

But she knew that portion of his body the sheet sheathed, knew it as intimately as he knew hers. She smiled at the memory. She longed to wake him and renew what they'd shared last night, but he looked so perfect, so peaceful in sleep. Quietly she slipped from his bed.

Finding the dress shirt he'd worn yesterday, she put it on, wrapping herself in the softness of the fabric, the male scent of him. She curled up in the big, overstuffed chair beside the bed and tucked her legs under her to watch him sleep.

Whenever intimations of good sense intruded, she quickly shoved them aside. There'd be plenty of time for regret, self-recrimination later, when she had to return to Boston. For now she'd concentrate only on how right it had felt to be there in Nick's arms, how natural to make love with him.

Nick awoke to find Fiona sitting in the chair, his blue shirt draped sensuously over her, a faraway look in her eyes. The wonder of last night swept over him, the feel of her beautiful body, so tempting, so soft, so willing. She'd been a perfect lover.

"I like the way you look in my shirt," he murmured. She hadn't buttoned it and the edge of one kiss-swollen breast peeked out. His body hardened with wanting her again. "Spend the day with me," he said, not able to bear the thought of a moment away from her.

"The day? You don't have to go into the office?"

He shook his head. "It's Saturday."

So it was. Fiona had lost all track of time since she'd come to Nevada, one day blending into the next. But *this* day she very much wanted to spend with Nick.

They made love again—slow and languorous love. Nick drew it out until she was beyond all thought, all reason, before finally giving her what she craved.

They showered together, bathing each other and toweling each other dry with thick, thirsty towels. "If we're going to spend today together, I'll need clean clothes," Fiona announced.

"I kinda like the way you look in that towel myself." He planted a kiss on one bare shoulder, then the top of one breast.

She threw her head back, drinking in the pleasure of his mouth on her fresh-scrubbed skin. "Then you intend for us to stay in all day?"

She knew they had to put in an appearance at Winnie's. And Nick had mentioned a restaurant that made delicious pancakes.

Nick groaned. "It's tempting, *very* tempt-

"I'm afraid that in my father's golden years he's searching for something different, something other than what he had with my mother," she said.

"And you think that something different won't be as good."

"That it won't . . . last," she clarified.

Camille grew thoughtful. "You loved your mother very much. I can see how this would be hard for you."

Fiona batted at a "welcome home" balloon, fluttering at half-mast from its mooring at the back of her chair. "And how do you feel, Camille?"

"Walter's sweet, precious. I liked him right away." She smiled. "And despite the fact that Nick thinks I should send my mother on an all-expenses-paid trip to the moon until she comes to her senses, I think they're going to do what they planned—get married. With or without our blessings."

Fiona nodded. Camille was no doubt right. Very right.

"But enough about their affair. I'm curious to know what's going on between you and that hunk of a cousin of mine." Camille's voice was low, hushed, urging girl-sharing confidences.

Fiona leaned back in her chair, maybe to distance herself from the question. "There's nothing going on."

Camille gave her a hard don't-expect-me-to-believe-that look. "I may have been out of the country, but I'm not out of touch with reality. And the looks that man's been sending you across the patio all evening are very *real*."

Fiona opened her mouth to deny it, but the truth was she'd caught Nick's gaze on her more than once. She'd wanted to wrap her body in its heat. Every inch of her tingled from it.

She'd sought him out, too. She'd known where he was every second of the evening, as if by some sort of feminine radar that the military could patent. But she wasn't ready to admit any of this to the all-too-perceptive Camille.

"I think you have an overactive imagination," she said, then punctuated her statement by scraping back her chair and offering Camille her best innocent smile. "I'm going to find a cold drink. Can I get one for you?"

Camille wasn't going to be dissuaded. "I'm seldom wrong. I know Nick very well, and you have him acting like he's been hit by a truck."

Fiona knew the feeling, but she didn't need to say so to Camille. Instead she turned toward the bar at the corner of the patio, leaving Camille grinning after her.

Halfway there, Nick intercepted her. "What's the matter with you? You look like you're trying to escape a firing squad."

Fiona glanced up into his tanned face. It

ing, but I'm not sure my body can take it, sweetheart."

She laughed softly.

After a quick trip to her hotel for clothes, then a breakfast of pancakes with pineapple syrup at Nick's favorite hangout, they drove by Winnie's.

Camille met them at the door. "Oh, you're just in time for brunch. I'm serving on the patio in five minutes," she said.

Nick and Fiona glanced at each other, then back at Camille. "We've, uh, already had breakfast," Nick told her.

Camille gave a knowing, catlike smile. "Together, no doubt. Well, join us for a glass of guava juice, anyway."

"Why did we have to come here?" Fiona asked Nick quietly once Camille had retreated to the kitchen.

"We had to check on Auntie."

"Ah yes—Auntie." Fiona only hoped Winnie wasn't as perceptive as her daughter. She suspected, though, that the truth of her and Nick's night together was stamped clearly on their faces.

The swelling in Winnie's ankle was down considerably this morning, no doubt because of Walter's loving, nursing care. "I'll be back on my feet in no time and ready for my wedding," she announced when they joined her and Fiona's father on the patio.

"That's wonderful," Fiona said, then saw Nick's jaw tighten and his shoulders take on a certain rigidity. His opinion about this wedding hadn't changed as hers had. He refused to see that the couple were in love—deeply in love.

A small sigh slipped from her lips. She knew that as long as his viewpoint remained overshadowed by his cases—and his past—there was no chance of a future for her with Nick.

After a polite length of time they slipped away, but before they'd gotten completely out of earshot, they heard Winnie say, "Oh, Walter, this is so wonderful. My Nicholas and your Fiona—a pair."

Fiona sighed again. Winnie had that only partially right.

"Get me away from here fast," she begged Nick.

He brushed a knuckle over her cheek. "I'm sorry my family is so intuitive. I didn't mean for them to embarrass you."

Once they were safely in the car, Nick turned to her. "How are you at sailing?" he asked.

Fiona relaxed against the seat and smiled. "I grew up beside the Atlantic, remember?"

"Ah, yes. Well, I keep a small boat out at Lake Mead. Are you game?"

That sounded like a good way to take her

mind off the differences between them. She nodded.

Sailing proved to be very distracting. Nick kept Fiona busy, helping to keep the craft upright in the choppy waters of the sparkling blue lake, but not so busy that she didn't have time to be haunted by the beauty of his tanned body, stripped to the waist.

His muscles bunched and rippled as he trimmed the sails, the sun glinted on his sleek, sweating torso, and Fiona couldn't take her eyes off of him.

Their night proved to be as active as their day. They made love, losing themselves in each other again.

The following day they hiked the mountain trails. Nick collected wildflowers and presented them to her, claiming the scent of them reminded him of her.

The smell of the flowers reminded Fiona instead of this desert paradise, the place where Nick very much belonged. And they reminded her of weddings.

Would Winnie carry a small bouquet of these desert blooms at her wedding? she wondered. Or something more traditional?

She sighed, wishing she knew how to convince Nick of the couple's love, wishing she could make him see that her father only wanted to make Winnie happy, that they would love each other for all time.

But Nick couldn't believe—wouldn't believe—that marriages could last. And flourish. And she knew that if she spoke the words of love that were in her heart, if she told Nick that she'd fallen crazily in love with him, he would only scoff.

Plucking a petal from the bouquet, she let it fall from her fingers.

That night they shared a candlelit supper at a nearby restaurant, then Nick returned her to her hotel. He had an early flight in the morning. To L.A. For yet another divorce case.

Fiona hated finding herself alone in bed, for what promised to be an endless night. She beat and pummeled her pillow, restless with wanting Nick.

"Better get used to it," she whispered aloud to herself.

But she feared her life had taken a turn from which she might never recover.

Fiona found herself at loose ends the next day without Nick, but Camille quickly remedied that.

"Without my cousin monopolizing your time, I thought you might help me shop for something to wear to my mother's wedding," she said in an early-morning call.

"Oh, Camille, I'd like that," Fiona replied. Lately her shopping consisted only of buying treasures for her antique shop, few for herself. But occasionally Elaine would drag her away from business to meander through the shops along Newbury Street or make a run through Filene's.

Shopping with Camille sounded like fun. And she found herself looking forward to it.

"Mother proclaimed my meager wardrobe abysmal, something even the charity closet wouldn't take," Camille groaned. "A fashionable wardrobe is not high on my list of needs in India, I'm afraid. I'm a bit rusty at choosing something appropriate for a garden wedding. I'd really appreciate your advice."

"Then you've got it."

Fiona had never had a sister to share things with, and she felt light and buoyant when she met Camille at the Fashion Mall an hour later. It was located on the Las Vegas Strip not far from her hotel, a sprawling mall with a wide variety of stores.

Fiona had forgotten to toss in her pink pumps when she'd hurriedly packed for this trip, so the two browsed through the multitude of shoe stores for just the pair to go with the pink suit she would wear to the wedding.

Fiona found the perfect linen ones, then

Camille talked her into trying on a pair of sexy strappy sandals as well. "What do you think?" Fiona asked, raising the skirt of her sundress and imitating a model's waltz across the shoe salon.

Camille gave a teasing smile. "I think they'll send my bachelor cousin into a male tailspin when he sees you in them."

Nick . . .

Fiona stared down at the seductive sandals for a long moment. Yes, he would find them tantalizing. They made her legs look endlessly long and her feet sexy and bare. But no matter how enticing she looked to Nick, it wouldn't change the basic problem in their relationship.

With a sigh she began to unbuckle the strap.

"What's wrong, Fiona? Don't you like them?"

Perhaps if she'd had a sister she would know how to share confidences, she'd know how to pour out her heart to Camille. But she'd never had a sister, and she didn't know how to tell Camille about the pain that speared through her.

She held the pair of sandals in her hands. "I'm not sure the shoes are all that practical. Boston has more winter weather than summer." And she would be returning home all too soon, she added to herself.

She was relieved when Camille bought her explanation.

"We'll have lunch. There's always time to come back and get them later if you change your mind," Camille said. "Come on, I know the perfect spot."

Perfect to Camille was a vegetarian restaurant, a purist way of life she'd adopted a long time ago. Fiona wasn't into bean sprouts and varieties of endive but managed to find a vegetarian pizza on the menu, topped with enough cheese to satisfy her taste buds.

Then it was on to more stores and a dozen boutiques to find a dress that would please Camille's mother, yet cater to Camille's bohemian style. By the end of the day she'd settled on one, a flouncy-skirted confection, sprigged with splashes of flowers. She'd even decided to leave off her Birkenstocks and stuff her feet into a conventional dainty pair of heels for the occasion.

"Oh, Fiona, I've had such a wonderful day. You don't know how terrific it is to have a sister at long last."

Fiona hugged her. "Oh, yes, I do. Now. I grew up an only child. But you at least had Nick."

Camille linked her arm with Fiona's. "In a way, yes. But Nick was always a bit of a loner. He never talked about it much, but he's always carried around a lot of pain in his heart."

"His mother's death?"

Camille nodded. "That and his father abandoning him."

"Oh, how horrible. I didn't know. He never mentioned his father."

"My parents showered him with love; that's why he's so devoted to his aunt Winnie, but he never had . . . I don't know . . . a sense of permanence in his life."

And he didn't see it in the cases he tried, Fiona knew. He saw the worst of human nature.

She wanted to heal him with her own love, kiss away his doubts. But could she? Was it possible?

TEN

The day of the wedding had finally arrived. Fiona helped Winnie and Camille put on the last-minute finishing touches.

Her father was no help at all; he just paced the patio and generally looked confused with all the hubbub going on around him.

Fiona gave him a hug. "Having second thoughts about the wedding, Dad?"

"Of course not," he replied. "You're not going to start in on that again, are you, Fiona?"

"No, Dad, I'm not going to start in on anything. It's just that you seem . . . well, nervous."

"Every man's jittery on his wedding day. We're supposed to be," he blustered.

She arched an eyebrow at him. "Is that some unwritten male law?"

He waved off her question. "Fiona, go and help Winnie with all that fussing she's doing and leave me to pace in peace."

She smiled and gave him a quick peck on his leathery cheek, then went off in search of a chore that needed doing.

Nick had promised to come by Winnie's this morning, but he hadn't shown up. And Fiona knew why. He still felt the same way about this wedding, but he loved his aunt too much to rain on her parade, so he was keeping his distance until the last minute.

Over the past few days Fiona and Nick had spent every spare moment they could together. Nick's caseload had been heavy, but they still managed to steal away for private interludes. Fiona had refused to think about the time when she'd have to leave and return to Boston. Leave Nick and the wonder of their lovemaking.

The antiques that were her life, the shop that was her fledgling baby, paled in comparison to the thought of staying. But very soon she would need that shop and its challenges to help her forget Nick and how he could make her body sing from just his touch, his kiss.

Somehow she'd have to relegate him to memory, a memory so bittersweet that just recalling it would cause her pain. A memory that would be stirred up again each time there was a family gathering.

For her sanity she hoped the distance across the country would keep those inevitable gatherings to a minimum.

"Oh, Fiona darling, there you are," Winnie called to her. She was dressed in a brightly colored caftan, her hair in curlers, but she had that radiant glow, common to all brides on their wedding day. "I want us to talk."

"Talk?"

"Yes. Let's find a quiet corner."

Winnie ushered her away from the commotion with the caterers and florists and into her bedroom, the bedroom Fiona's father would soon be sharing with his new bride.

Fiona tried not to glance around the room too much. Winnie had come into her father's affections like a small desert tornado. And Fiona thought she had resigned herself to that, and to the wedding that would take place in a few short hours.

But suddenly she didn't know what to do with her memories of the past, those quick, fragile images she had of her parents together, laughing, touching hands, kissing each other good night.

Where did she tuck them away?

Winnie patted a spot on the bed. "Sit, Fiona," she said.

Fiona hesitated for a moment, then took the place Winnie indicated beside her.

"I thought we might have a little talk,

Fiona," Winnie began. "Just the two of us. A sort of . . . mother-daughter talk."

A mother-daughter talk? Fiona hoped Winnie wasn't about to ask her to call her mother. She'd grown fond of Winnie, very fond. She was going to be her father's new wife, and Fiona approved of that. Her mother was gone, and life marched on, Fiona knew. But the woman who'd given her birth, who'd loved her through braces, her first date, and school proms, was special. Fiona wasn't sure she could ever share the title.

"Yes, Winnie?" She knew she'd stressed the name as if to ward off the other possible appellation.

Winnie took Fiona's hands in hers. "Walter has told me how close you and your mother were, and dear, I just want you to know that I'll never intrude on those memories. Or those of your father's with her. Those are precious to you. And to him."

Fiona felt quick tears glisten in her eyes, threatening to spill over—not at the mention of her mother, but at the understanding and gentle sensitivity she'd found in Winnie.

"I have my memories of Gray, the same way your father does of Elise," she went on when Fiona couldn't find her voice around the lump that had begun to swell in her throat. "Walter and I agreed we would respect each other's past marriages and we prayed our children would be accepting of our new relationship."

Fiona was near breaking.

"I won't try to replace your mother, Fiona, but I hope you'll let me into your heart—just one small corner of it."

"Oh, Winnie." Fiona couldn't say more; she only embraced this woman who was making such big changes in everyone's life.

Any last niggling doubt for her father's future happiness with this woman melted away. Winnie was just the woman her father needed in his golden years. Maybe Fiona would never be able to call her mother, but there was definitely a special place for her in her heart.

When her tears abated, Fiona glanced up into Winnie's wonderful, wise face. "It's easy to see why my father loves you," she said. "And, yes, I very much approve of your relationship, and your wedding. I wish you both the very best. Forever."

The two women hugged again.

The guests had begun to arrive for the ceremony, dressed in their garden-party finery, filling the white wooden folding chairs set up on the lawn near the flower-festooned gazebo. Winnie had learned her lesson about climbing on stepladders and had left that decorating detail to a bevy of florists.

Camille was helping Winnie dress. Fiona was trying to calm her father with his inevitable bridegroom jitters. And Nick was nowhere in sight.

Fiona's stomach clenched. She could hardly believe Nick would be so unreasonable that he wouldn't come to the wedding. But he wasn't here.

"How's Win?" her father asked for the third time in the past hour.

"I told you she's fine, Dad. She's dressing."

"Well, I don't know who thought of this silly rule that a man can't see his bride in her wedding dress until the ceremony."

Fiona hid a smile. "Probably the same one who said the bridegroom was supposed to be nervous."

"Yeah, well . . ." He didn't have a comeback this time. Instead he turned all serious on her. "Fiona, are you okay with this wedding thing? I mean, your mother and I . . . well, we had a good life together, a wonderful life together, and I . . ." He paused, clearly struggling. "Oh, Fiona, I'm not very good at talking about this feeling stuff. What I'm saying is . . ."

She reached up and kissed his cheek. "I'm fine with this wedding stuff, Dad. Winnie and I had a little talk earlier. I think she's one very

Here Comes the Bride

special lady. And you're one lucky guy to have found her."

"You and Win had a talk, huh?" He beamed. "You women know how to do that sort of thing." He looked pleased that he could retreat back into his comfortable, old-fashioned image of a man's duties in life.

But Fiona loved him despite it.

Just then there was a flurry of activity. The music started and last-minute arrivals hurried to take their seats. Winnie stood poised at the patio door, ready to make her entrance.

Fiona took one last frantic glance around for Nick. He still wasn't there. A myriad of emotions ripped through her, disappointment that he could be so unfeeling being the major one. This would devastate Winnie.

With an ache in her heart, she kissed her father one last time, wished him luck, and sent him to his post at the front of the gazebo to await his bride.

She turned to find her place as the music segued into the "Wedding March." Again she searched for Nick, wishing she were some kind of genie who could conjure him up at will.

And then she saw him.

Fiona knew at that moment that all eyes were supposed to be on the bride, but hers were on Nick. He stood at the edge of the patio, tall and square-shouldered in his white tux, stunning and elegant and all male.

Her breath caught in her throat.

Briefly he scanned the group, then finding her, he paused. Their gazes locked and held. She tried to read his face, but his expression was inscrutable.

The music swelled and he turned away to offer his arm to Winnie for her walk down the aisle.

Fiona's heart thudded. Shaky, she slid into her chair.

Nick's escorting of Winnie had not been part of the rehearsal. The woman, with her feisty independence, had insisted she could make it under her own steam quite nicely. But Nick apparently had other ideas, Fiona thought with a smile.

She knew he had not changed his mind about this wedding, but if Winnie was determined to go through with it, he, Nick, would do the honors.

Winnie had her face turned upward to his, her eyes widening for a moment, but she accepted his arm. When they reached the gazebo, Nick placed Winnie's hand in Walter's, then stepped aside.

His face remained unreadable as he took his seat beside Fiona and Camille, but Fiona knew what this had cost him emotionally.

The wedding was called a success by everyone—with the possible exception of Nick.

Fiona was happy for the couple, who hadn't taken their eyes off each other since the *I do*'s. She and Camille had dabbed at their eyes throughout the ceremony, snuffling back tears, while Nick remained dry-eyed and silent beside them.

The patio reception hummed around her as she searched out Nick. Only a few moments before she'd seen him listening distractedly to a lady in a turquoise-plumed hat. Fiona saw the feather bob through the crowd as the lady made her way to the champagne table, but Nick was nowhere in sight.

She scanned the group again. Then she spotted him, standing alone and aloof, near a leg of the striped canopy that draped the patio as if he were personally responsible for holding it up.

In all the excitement of the wedding, they hadn't had a moment to exchange a word. He was troubled, and she wanted to chase away his demons, but she wasn't sure how to do it, how to make him believe in a world of happiness, that such a world was possible for Walter and Winnie, that it was possible for *them*.

With a deep sigh she made her way toward him.

Nick took another swallow of his champagne, but the bubbly had failed to put him in a festive mood. Then he spotted Fiona as she made her way through the crowded reception, clearly headed in his direction.

Her flame-red hair tumbled over the shoulders of her sleek linen suit and down her back. The day he'd first seen her in the airport, he'd thought she looked stunning in white, but pink came a damned close second. Whoever said redheads couldn't wear the color had never seen Fiona Ames.

He ached with his need for her. All through the ceremony he'd wanted to snatch her away from the place, wanted to drown himself in the taunting, flowery scent of her.

He wanted her to make him believe love existed. Somewhere. For some people.

For Fiona and him.

"Care to buy a lady a drink?"

Fiona's green eyes smiled up at him. His heart turned over. Her lips were moist and sultry pink. And he wanted to kiss them, savor them, feel them dance over his body as they had the past few nights.

But the lady had asked for a drink—not a trip to the bedroom.

"Right this way." He took her hand and led her toward the champagne table.

Her fingers, so delicate and slender, felt lost in his grasp. His hand closed tighter around them as he drew her through the gathering. Occasionally someone stopped them to speak or say hello. Nick wasn't in the mood to share her with anyone. He suspected they had very little time left together, but that was a fact he wasn't capable of facing yet.

They'd reached the table. The cascading champagne fountain gave off a fine mist in the light, outdoor breeze. Nick filled a flute for her, then his own near-empty one. "Let's get away from the jostle of the crowd," he said.

She agreed and allowed him to guide her out onto the lawn. Here the air was pleasant, musky and cool, as the evening gave way to night. Nick still had Fiona's hand in his and he brought it to his lips. Her dark lashes fluttered in reaction and he liked it that he could affect her so.

"You look beautiful," he murmured. "Soft, like a fresh, pink flower."

She smiled, then fingered a pearl stud on the front of his shirt, first one, then another, making her way slowly down. "You look pretty nice yourself," she returned.

He caught her hand before she went lower. Didn't she know how she set him on fire?

He took a swallow of champagne.

Fiona sipped hers, then she glanced up. "That was a nice gesture before, Nick. Walking Winnie down the aisle."

He lowered his gaze. "Yeah, well . . ."

"Well, what?"

He turned and paced a short distance across the lawn, crushing the thick carpet of grass beneath his shoes. "Do we have to talk about it? The deed is done."

Fiona heard the pain in his voice. His emotions ran deep. She'd thought—*hoped*—that after the ceremony he'd be more accepting of the marriage. That obviously hadn't happened.

And wouldn't.

She took a step toward him and touched his arm, hating the way the brooding moment seemed to separate them.

He turned toward her and gazed at her for a long moment. Raising his hand, he stroked her cheek. "I—I was married once, Fiona," he said quietly. His voice was low, a bare whisper in the night. "Everyone toasted us, the bride was beautiful, and I thought life would finally be complete for me. But like other things in my life, it didn't happen."

Fiona heard the pain that throbbed in his voice. "What other things in your life, Nick? Your mother's death? Your father abandoning you?"

His eyes widened in surprise. "Who told you about my father? Camille?"

"Yes."

Nick never spoke of the man, tried never

Here Comes the Bride

to think of him, but he was always there, hovering just at the frayed edges of his memory, he and the hurt he'd caused. "That was a long time ago, Fiona."

"Maybe—but it still hurts you."

"Only if I allow it to." Lifting his champagne glass, he took a hard swallow. He'd barely lowered the glass when Fiona reached up and kissed him lightly on the mouth, a mere brush of her lips, but she tasted like an oasis in the desert.

His eyes closed, and for one wondrous moment he almost believed she could be just that—his oasis. That she could make him believe in forever.

That it was possible.

The reception drew to an end when the wedding couple departed, ducking into a limousine in a shower of rice. They were spending the night in the bridal suite at Caesar's, then taking off in the morning for a two-week trip in Walter's old sedan. He'd been polishing it for days.

Nick groaned just thinking of it, and hoped the car didn't leave Auntie stranded by the side of the road in some desolate location. Just because she was married to Walter didn't relieve him of responsibility for her welfare.

When the last guest had departed, Nick

and Fiona and Camille heaved a collective sigh.

"Wasn't that just the most *beautiful* wedding?" Camille exclaimed, plucking a bright pink floribunda and sniffing it delicately.

"As weddings go," Nick returned. His cousin had a dreamy, faraway look in her eyes, as if she'd been caught up in a fairy tale.

Fiona wore the same look of unreality.

Why did women gush over weddings? What was it about them that brought fatuous smiles to their lips and made them cry over the bride and groom with such happiness?

Nick knew how quickly fairy-tale marriages could end. He was the one who picked up the pieces of these people's lives later.

"Let's get this place cleaned up," he said, looking around at the aftermath of the celebration.

Fiona didn't want to go back to the hotel. She was too excited to sleep. Besides, she didn't want tomorrow to come.

Tomorrow Camille was leaving, returning to India. And Fiona had to get back to Boston and her shop. Tomorrow she'd have to say good-bye to Nick.

It was a day she'd put off thinking about.

"Could we drive for a while?" she asked

him as he pulled the Porsche away from Winnie's house.

"Drive?" He turned to glance at her.

"Yes. I know I won't be able to sleep a wink, not with all the excitement of the evening still tripping through my brain. Unless, of course, you're too tired," she added. Nick had done most of the cleanup around Winnie's and it had been a long day for everyone. She was being inconsiderate. Still, she hoped he'd say yes.

"I don't feel sleepy myself. Sure, let's drive. Anyplace in particular?"

"Nope." She settled back in the seat, letting the wind blow her hair every which way. It would be hopelessly tangled, but tonight she didn't care.

Her life was just as hopelessly tangled. And she didn't care about that either. Or at least she refused to think about it. There'd be plenty of time to reflect on the impossibility of her situation with Nick once she returned to Boston.

If this was their last night together, she didn't want to ruin it with desperation.

They'd both changed out of their wedding finery earlier. She'd shed the linen suit, slipping back into her shorts and a T-shirt for the cleanup. Nick, too, had changed out of his tux into form-hugging jeans and a black knit polo.

Fiona had hardly been able to keep her

eyes off him all evening. He'd looked devastating in his white tux, elegant, aloof . . . untouchable. He looked just as untouchable now. She wanted to reach over and kiss him, tell him everything would be okay with Winnie and Walter. She wanted to tell him that life wasn't always the way he encountered it.

Love, strong and sure and unwavering, did happen to people. And when it did, it should be celebrated, not viewed with doubt and skepticism.

Fiona had been a doubter, too, when she'd come to Las Vegas, so sure her father could not have fallen in love with Winnie so quickly. But love, she found out, didn't adhere to timetables.

She'd fallen in love with Nick in just as short a span of time. Crazy, she knew, but it was true—hopelessly true.

They had left the town behind. Nothing but desert stretched ahead of them, its dark, barren beauty marred only by the headlights of an occasional oncoming car. Neither of them had spoken for the past dozen miles, each pensively lost in his own thoughts.

Nick's face gleamed hard and lean with the moonlight slanting across it as he drove. There was a tension in him Fiona longed to kiss away. She wanted to run her hands over his hard, bare shoulders and down his taut arms until they grew relaxed and he reached for her. She wanted to press her mouth to his and wipe away the years of pain and hurt Winnie and Gray had tried to erase with their love and nurturing.

She wanted to love away all the hopelessness he encountered daily in people's lives, hopelessness that was beyond him to repair, but that, nonetheless, ate at him and threatened any future happiness.

Tall order, Fiona, she told herself.

What made her think she could succeed where others had failed? She sighed and hugged her arms to herself.

"Cold?" Nick asked, glancing over at her. "I have a sweatshirt in the trunk."

"No, I'm fine." The warmth of a sweatshirt couldn't help her. It couldn't ward off the chill of a future without Nick.

Their drive had taken them to Lake Mead, where they'd sailed together a few days earlier. Memories of that day came flooding back to her, that day and all the others she'd spent with him since coming here.

She wanted more days with Nick—and more nights. She wanted this night. She wanted him to make love to her again—one last time. And she wanted to pretend it was forever.

"Nick, can we spend the night on the boat?"

Nick turned toward her and studied her

face in the pale moonlight. It was naked with longing, with want. If he lived to be a thousand, he'd never forget the way this lady could proposition him.

Nothing in his past—or his future—he was certain, could ever compare. Fiona was a haunting mixture of reticence and brazenness. One minute she was as old-fashioned as her name, believing in happily-ever-afters and crying at weddings, the next she was asking him to do wicked things to her body.

"The night, huh?" That was an offer no sane man could refuse, though he knew, for her sake—for his—he should. "I know a nice, private cove."

ELEVEN

"Do . . . you come here often?" Fiona asked once Nick dropped anchor.

The cove was more than private. It was a haven. The moon and the stars were their only neighbors. And silence, silence broken only by the waves lapping softly against the hull, and more distantly, the shoreline, perhaps ten feet away. An intimate place, a place for making love.

Nick came over to her and took her face between his hands. "If you're asking if I bring my women here, the answer is no. You're the first."

A shiver climbed her spine. His reply pleased her. "I—I'm glad you thought of it." She'd die before she'd admit that was the very question on the tip of her tongue.

"Oh, *this*, lady, was entirely your idea." He smiled wickedly and caressed her nipple.

It sent a primitive pull to the core of her. "How gallant of you to remind me."

His smile only widened. He was mighty pleased with himself. What man didn't enjoy a proposition from a woman?

"I, uh, might have a bottle of wine onboard and I could scare us up some cheese," he said, still stroking her nipple through her shirt with infinite slowness.

What it was doing to her didn't put her in mind of eating . . . or sipping wine with him. Her appetites at the moment ran to a need more vital. "Forget the wine," she ordered.

He let out a purr of pleasure and cupped her bottom, then drew her hard against him. "I do believe the lady knows what she wants."

And it was no secret that he wanted the same thing. In fact, he was more than willing. Hot and ready for whatever she had in store for him. She wriggled against his hardness and heard his groan of agony.

"Any more of that and I'll pick you up and carry you below deck, woman," he murmured in a husky threat.

"No," she said. "I want you up here where I can see your body naked in the moonlight." She wanted to remember him that way, all silvery-sheened and male. "I want to feel the night on us, the breeze awakening our every nerve ending."

"Your hands are doing one helluva job of that already."

Fiona nearly had him out of his clothes, enjoying the feel of his skin beneath her touch. She memorized the texture of it, from rough to smooth to the velvet heat of his maleness.

He sucked in a breath when she touched him there and called her something that sounded like "witch." At least she hoped that was what she'd heard.

The boat rocked in a rhythm beneath them, making it seem like they were dancing. In a way, they were, a dance with music heard only by the two of them, music that would haunt her again and again when Nick was no longer in her life—when she was alone and aching for him.

Nick had stripped her of her clothes as well, teasing and tormenting her with his mouth, his tongue, in places he'd never found before, sending her spiraling into sweet ecstasy.

Then, as the night whispered around them and the moonlight touched their nakedness, they joined together, moving together in a fierceness that hadn't driven them before. Maybe because this was to be the last time. She obliterated that thought with the glory of him inside her and rose with him until she felt herself fragment into a million tiny shards of pleasure.

They spent the night on deck, wrapped together in a blanket Nick had stowed, sipping the wine he'd found. There'd been only one small wedge of cheese, but they'd shared it, feeding each other tiny bites.

They didn't sleep, only held each other and murmured all the wonderful things lovers say—everything, save one: *I love you.*

How could she say those words to a man who didn't believe in love?

Sitting up, she let the blanket fall and reached for her clothes. She needed space. She needed distance. She needed to clear her head —and her heart—of Nick.

Nick's hand shot out, pinning her to the spot. "Where do you think you're going?" he demanded. His hand cupped her breast, his fingers teasing her nipple lazily, seductively.

She wanted to slide down into the blanket next to him, let him do all the wondrous things to her body that he'd done earlier, but she knew this was the end, the end of all that they had shared. There was no future for her with Nick.

She'd known that from the beginning. But why, when faced with the reality of it now, did it hurt so damned much?

She wriggled her T-shirt over her head

Here Comes the Bride

and shimmied it down to cover her nakedness. Nick's hand fell to the bareness of her leg, his fingers trailing a seductive path up her thigh.

His touch was nearly her undoing. She struggled for strength. "It's almost morning," she said, and drew away, slipping hastily into her shorts.

"Yes, it's almost morning," Nick repeated.

She heard a catch to his voice, and then she knew that he, too, realized the full implication of that fact. Their time together was over.

"I'm leaving today," she added quietly.

She didn't look at him, but she could feel him recoil at her statement.

Say something, Nick, she cried inside. *Tell me to stay. Tell me you love me.* But even as her brain screamed the words she knew she wouldn't hear them, not from Nick.

She got up and paced across the deck. Golden fingers of light speared the waning night sky. If it were possible, she'd hold back the sunrise. Morning would never come.

Nick shucked off the confining blanket and yanked on his jeans. Fiona looked so tiny, so fragile, so beautiful, standing there, gazing out across the lake. He wanted to go to her, beg her to stay, but he knew he had nothing to offer her.

He'd come so close to falling in love with her, so close to believing it really did exist.

He'd listened to Auntie and Walter exchange their vows and tried desperately to believe.

He'd squeezed his eyes shut and tried to imagine himself and Fiona saying those words, promising forever to each other, but it was no good. Something was lacking in him. Faith had died in him a long time ago.

He wished he could go to her, pull her into his arms, and tell her she belonged to him, *tell her he loved her*, but the words would sound foreign, hollow.

He crossed the deck to her and coiled a silken strand of her tangled hair around his finger. He didn't dare touch any other part of her. "When does your plane leave?" he asked.

He felt her body grow taut. It had been a simple question, and not so simple. With it, he'd condemned their relationship to its end.

He wanted to yank back the words. If only he and Fiona had had more time, but he knew that would not have solved anything between them, only made it that much harder to part.

"It's a one-thirty flight," she managed to say. There was a quaver in her voice and he wished he could kiss it away from her throat.

He was hurting her, he knew, but if he asked her to stay, he'd only hurt her more. He couldn't be what she needed. "I'll see what there is in the galley for breakfast."

"No." She put a staying hand on his arm, then quickly withdrew it as if she'd been burned. "Nick, I'd like to go back to the hotel. I . . . I need to pack."

Nick studied her for a long moment. "Are you sure?"

"I'm sure."

Everything else between them went unsaid.

"What's the matter with you two? You both look like you just lost your best friend," Camille remarked, her gaze sliding over Nick first, then Fiona, her perception rapier-sharp.

They'd stopped by Winnie's on the way in from Lake Mead so Fiona could say good-bye to Camille, but she hadn't considered how close to the surface their emotions shimmered.

"Something like that," Nick said. He shared a glance with Fiona, then frowned and sauntered away, off to the kitchen, no doubt to find something for breakfast. Neither he nor Fiona had eaten—and Fiona wasn't sure she ever would again.

She smiled wanly at Camille, not knowing what to say. A tight knot of emotion threatened to close off her throat. "We had, uh . . ."

"A lovers' quarrel?" Camille supplied.

Fiona shook her head. "No, not a quarrel." She could use a friendly shoulder to cry on right now—and Camille had become both friend and sister these past few days—but Fiona didn't dare let her feelings show right now. She didn't dare do so until she was back home and alone with her pain.

She raised her chin high and forced a courageous smile. "Nick and I, well, we decided things can't work out for us."

"*Fiona!*"

Fiona went on in spite of Camille's protest. "It's time for me to go home. I've abandoned my shop for far too long, as it is." Elaine had told her her customers were being very understanding, when she had called, but she needed to be there. She needed the shop's familiar warmth and security. "I—I'm leaving this afternoon, Camille."

Camille studied her for a long moment, as if she couldn't quite accept the reality of what was happening. "Mother and Walter will be disappointed," she said. "They were ecstatic when you and Nick—"

"They were just ecstatic period," Fiona pointed out. "They're in love and they want the whole world to be." And not everyone could be; she knew that.

Camille sighed. "I had my hopes, too, that things would work out for you and my bachelor cousin. I'd hoped there would be another wedding for me to come home for very soon."

"Well, you were wrong."

"Maybe, maybe not. Whether Nick knows it or not, he needs you. He needs to know that love, the kind of love he can have with you, exists. He's buried himself in those horrid divorce cases for so long, it's warped him to everything beautiful in the world. You're what Nick needs, Fiona. You're perfect for him."

"No, not perfect, Camille. Someone perfect would know how to heal him. I—I don't know how to do that."

Camille reached out and wrapped her arms around Fiona in a sisterly embrace. "I'm going back to India because it's what I want, what's right for me. Are you sure you're doing what's right for you, Fiona?"

Fiona couldn't answer. She swallowed a lump in her throat the size of a mountain.

Tossing the last item into her suitcase, Fiona glanced around the room to see if she'd left anything behind. Only her heart, she thought sadly.

She wouldn't cry—she'd promised herself that.

She'd held back the tears with Camille. She'd held back the tears with Nick. He'd wanted to drive her to the airport, but she'd refused his offer. She wasn't sure she could hold up to any more good-byes.

Camille was leaving today too. She'd be

taking the night flight to New York, then on to India. Fiona wished they'd had more time to spend together, more time to cement the new sisterly relationship between them.

She wished she could have learned more about the work Camille was doing abroad and about the passion and excitement she felt for that work. Camille seemed to know what she wanted—and Fiona envied her that strength of purpose. She was sure one day Camille would find someone to love, someone to share her nomadic life with.

Perhaps, in time, Nick would find someone, too, someone who could make him believe in a whole and complete love. It hurt to think of him in another woman's arms. She squeezed her eyes shut to hold back the tears.

When she felt composed again, she picked up her bag, slung her purse strap over one shoulder, and started for the lobby—and a waiting cab.

"Taxi, lady?"

Nick stood beside the Porsche, smiling that smile she would always remember. For one wild moment her heart soared with the hope that he'd come to carry her off with him, but her head knew he'd merely changed his mind about letting her go to the airport alone.

Didn't he realize he was only making things harder for them both? "I'm not sure I can afford your price," she answered in truth.

She wasn't sure she could afford the cost in emotion.

He studied her solemnly for a quiet moment, then he snatched up her luggage and made room for it in the trunk of the car.

"Nick, you don't have to do this, you don't have to take me to the airport. I'm a big girl now."

"I know."

She'd wanted him to know she'd be okay about this, she'd be okay about everything. Or perhaps she'd wanted to convince herself. Whatever, he didn't owe her anything.

She'd gone into this brief relationship with her eyes wide open. And she had them open now. She retained no illusions about Nick—or about how difficult the weeks ahead would be without him.

They drove in silence for a few awkward miles. Fiona played with her purse strap and pretended a consuming interest in road signs.

Finally Nick turned to her. "Maybe you should stay a few days," he said. "I mean, what if Walter and Auntie don't hit it off? What if they don't last out the honeymoon?"

A worry line creased his forehead. Fiona knew this man, knew the feel of his skin, the taste of his mouth, the glory of his hands on her, and she died a thousand times inside at the keen realization that she'd never experience him again.

"Nick, Winnie and Walter will make it through their honeymoon and, I daresay, twenty years of wedded bliss. You don't have to worry about them." If only he wanted her to stay for other reasons, if only he believed they, too, could be that happy together.

That thought occupied her mind until Nick had parked and they were inside the terminal. "You don't have to go to the gate with me," she said once she'd checked her luggage and gotten her boarding pass.

"I know." Taking her arm, he led her toward the escalator.

They talked about phoning each other—concerning their relatives' well-being, of course; they talked about the weather back in Boston, and didn't she want a few snacks to take on the flight with her? But they didn't talk about what was going on inside each of them at that moment. That would have been too painful.

Finally Fiona's flight was called.

"Well, I guess this is it," she said. She shouldered her purse and put out her hand. "Good-bye, Nick."

But a handshake was far from good enough for Nick. He hauled her into his arms and kissed her hair, her cheek, then found her mouth, closing over it with the unmistakable taste of regret.

She soaked up the male heat of him one

last time. Her heart hammered until she thought it would splinter. An ache coupled with the pain of loss ripped through her, tearing at her insides. She loved this man, but love was not enough.

Blind with unshed tears, she tore herself away from him and escaped through the door and onto the jetway without a backward glance.

Nick frowned down at the contract he'd been reviewing for a client, then shoved the pages aside. He hadn't concentrated on a word of it since *the party of the first part.* In fact, he hadn't concentrated on much of anything in the past week and a half. Not since Fiona had gone back to Boston.

He'd turned down three major divorce cases because he was certain, in his present condition, he wouldn't be able to do them justice. Was that really it? he wondered. Concern for his illustrious—and winning—track record?

Or was it that he no longer had the stomach for watching couples who'd once professed undying love tear each other apart in the courtroom.

Maybe what he needed was a rest from work. How long had it been since he'd taken a vacation? He couldn't remember the last time.

The more he thought about it, the more the idea appealed to him. He leaned back in his desk chair and studied a wooden beam in the ceiling. Maybe he'd take a gambling junket to Nassau—or Atlantic City. A change of pace from Vegas.

He crossed one long leg over the other on the corner of his desk and wondered just how far Atlantic City was from Boston.

"Forget it, Killian," he muttered aloud. "What you had with the lady is over. She won't want to see you again."

"Talking to yourself now?"

Nick jerked to an upright position as Jasmine strode unannounced, and definitely uninvited, into his office. She dropped a stack of papers beside the rest of his unfinished work on the desk. "I wasn't talking to myself. I was . . . thinking out loud."

Jas merely raised an eyebrow at that. "Same difference."

He offered her a scowl, then snapped up the contract he'd been reading earlier and pretended busy interest.

"Is that thing written in Sanskrit or something?" She folded her arms in front of her and pursed her lips like a schoolteacher. "You were on that same page when I went to lunch —*over an hour ago.*"

Nick pushed back from his desk, plotting which way of firing her he'd enjoy best. "Is there some point you want to make or did you just come in here to harass me?"

She sat down opposite him, crossed one trim leg over the other, and smiled, quite pleased with herself. "What point could I possibly have to make? Just because you've been working at a pace a retarded snail could top ever since Fiona Ames blew this town . . ."

Maybe he could still get Jas her old job back, he thought crossly. "The pace I work at has nothing to do with Fiona." Just saying her name hurt like hell. Thinking about her nearly killed him. And the dreams he had— "Isn't there something you have to do at that desk of yours?"

"Not since the boss went into a major funk over the only woman who's mattered to him since I can't remember when," she retorted in that know-it-all, superior tone he'd rather not endure.

"Who made you an authority on the females in my life, may I ask?" Jas was hitting too close to a nerve. Hell, she was doing a tap dance on it with spiked shoes, but he'd be damned if he'd admit it to her.

"I'm just being a good little secretary." She stood up, riffled through the stack of papers she'd brought him, then shoved a neatly printed brochure in front of him. "Something you might want to attend," she said, tapping it mysteriously with the tip of one red nail.

Nick frowned and picked up the pamphlet. A legal seminar? He avoided them like the plague. He started to chuck it into his favorite circular file, then caught sight of the seminar's location—Boston, Massachusetts.

He studied the thing for one long, prurient moment, then shoved it into the wastebasket. If he wanted to see Fiona, he wouldn't hide behind a flimsy excuse like a seminar. He started to tell Jas just that, but when he glanced up, she was sashaying neatly out the door, apparently satisfied with her dirty work.

TWELVE

July had sweltered its way into Boston. Mornings were the only respite Fiona had from the heat—and they were short-lived. This accounted for her cross-patch humor, she told herself, determined to believe it. But each night she recognized it for the lie that it was.

At night she tossed and turned in her big, empty antique four-poster and missed Nick with a hunger she couldn't deny. Her memory betrayed her with its keen sense of detail, its sharp particulars of the silvery nights she'd had with Nick, the glorious days.

It had all felt so right at the time, but that sense of rightness had blinded her to the future—and the fact that there'd never be one with Nick.

She knew full well how he felt about love, about marriage. Nick had been perfectly honest about that.

It hurt to think of him, to remember his touch, his kiss, but still she couldn't summon up regret for the time she'd spent in his arms. What they'd shared had been special—even if Nick didn't realize it.

Time would ease her pain, make her memories of him more bearable. Time etched a patina on the antiques she sold in her shop, and time would etch a patina on her love for Nick too. One day she'd place that love on a shelf, cherished and beautiful, but relegated to the past.

One day it wouldn't hurt anymore.

Her hands dusty, she unpacked another new treasure she'd bought today at an auction in the country, carefully lifting it from its bed of protective newspapers. It was an old tarnished brass kaleidoscope, its antique stand broken, but it still worked. She raised it to the light and carefully rotated the cylinder, awed at the brilliant bursts of colors that emerged in front of her eyes.

Finally she set the piece aside and jotted it down on her inventory list. After adding the price she'd paid for it, she reached for the next item. But before she could unearth it, the bell over the shop door tinkled merrily. Glancing up, she saw Elaine from the photography shop next door breeze inside.

"The postman left your mail at my place while you were out antiquing this morning," she sang out. She threaded her way along the crowded, narrow aisle to the back.

"Thanks, Elaine." Fiona reached for it, but Elaine held it aloft, just out of reach.

"Not so fast," she said with a wide grin. "Who's Nick?"

"Nick?" Fiona's heart did a fast somersault. Had Nick written?

She hadn't heard from him since she'd been home. Several times she'd been tempted to call him—to see if he'd had any news of the delinquent honeymooners—but each time she'd thought better of it.

Hearing his voice would cause her fresh pain. She had to wait until she was stronger—until it would no longer hurt.

When Elaine began to read the postcard in her hand, Fiona realized it wasn't from Nick, but from her father and Winnie—*about* Nick.

Her heart sank as Elaine read aloud:

Dear Fiona,
Suppose by now you had to get back to your shop, but we hope not before you and Nick fell crazy in love. Don't mean to be nosy—it's just that we're so wildly happy, we want the same for those around us.
Talk to you both soon.
                  Love,
                  Walter and Winnie

Elaine raised her head from the card, her eyes shining with a speculative gleam. "I repeat my question. Who's Nick?"

Fiona dropped into an old Windsor chair she intended to refinish and let out a pent-up breath. Elaine was her closest friend in Boston —but she wasn't sure she could share the deepest part of her heart right now.

He wasn't needed.

Nick nursed the last of his scotch, then picked up the postcard he'd gotten from Auntie and read it through again.

She and Walter were happy. There was a glow to her words he'd have to have been blind to miss. She didn't need Nick to race to her rescue. The old sedan had even held up. Walter had wheeled it through the mountains at Tahoe without any trouble.

He got up and paced his condo that lately seemed to close in on him. He'd gotten away for a vacation, but after his second day in Nassau, he'd been so restless, he'd caught the next flight back to Vegas.

He'd missed Fiona too much while he was there—whenever he'd looked at a sunset, when he'd crawled into bed at night, and all the times in between.

When he'd returned, he'd checked in at his office, only to have Jas tell him the parties

Here Comes the Bride

of one of the divorce cases he'd been handling had reconciled in his absence.

He always recommended a cooling-off period to his clients, along with some stiff marriage counseling, but those measures seldom panned out.

Until now.

He didn't mind in the least losing the fat fee, but the turn of events had rattled his belief system.

And now Auntie's postcard was having the same cataclysmic effect on him. Love did seem to be alive and flourishing in the world, at least for a few.

Was it possible it could be that way for Fiona and him? Could he give her the kind of marriage she deserved, the forever kind?

He poured himself another drink, splashed in two ice cubes, and studied the amber liquid for the answer.

The midnight flight was full. Nick was squashed into a middle seat, the only one left on the crowded DC-9. He squirmed, trying to get comfortable between the two men on either side of him. The one by the window snored and the other wanted to talk.

Nick didn't want conversation. He wanted to count the miles, estimate the time down to the second that it would take him to get to Boston.

He chatted with the man on the aisle for a brief moment, his answers bordering on rudeness, though his seat companion didn't seem to notice. He was far too intent on relating to Nick the details of his winning streak that had turned sour.

Nick had heard the story before, a hundred different versions of it, but always with the same ending. People thought they could beat the odds. They couldn't.

And what about his own odds? Nick wondered. He had a lot more at stake here than a few measly gambling dollars. He was betting on the rest of his life.

By the time the plane touched down at Logan International, Nick had a bad case of nerves. After a quick shower and a change of clothes at the hotel, he walked over to Antiques 'n Such.

He had no trouble recognizing Fiona's shop. It was just as she'd described it to him, right down to the quaint copper kettle filled with bright flowers that hung out over the door.

The store's front window was stuffed with treasures, everything from an old grandfather clock to a child's rocking horse. The place echoed Fiona's uniqueness, her style and charm, her elegance and warmth. He stood across the tree-lined street and observed it all.

He wasn't sure she'd even want to see him. And he wouldn't blame her if she didn't. They hadn't talked of love. But Nick had felt it, with every touch, every caress, though it had scared the hell out of him at the time. It still did—enough to make him consider hopping the next plane back home.

Fiona had a life here in Boston, a life she loved, judging by the care and effort she'd put into her small shop. What did he have to offer her? Did he have the right to offer her *anything*? Perhaps she'd chosen to forget him, forget about their nights together in the desert.

All he knew was that he had to see her again, had to know if what they'd shared had been real. If there was a chance for them.

He crossed the street, wishing he had some small gift to bring her. He remembered how her eyes had lit up at the sight of the small antique jewelry box he'd bought for her that day they'd visited the ghost town together. He remembered his own pleasure at her surprise, her happiness.

He wished he had something now, something he could give her, something that would make her eyes light again even slightly. But he'd come to Boston totally unprepared. He'd hopped the first available flight without a thought for anything beyond seeing her again.

Then he spotted a vendor on the street corner selling flowers from a pushcart. What woman could resist flowers? He hoped Fiona couldn't, hoped it would soften her heart just a little, enough that she would listen to what he needed to say to her, what was in his heart. He raced off down the street.

"Got some pretty summer bouquets here," the flower woman said when he approached. "Fresh-picked blooms."

"Very pretty." Nick gazed over the selection. What kind would Fiona like? He didn't know. "Blue," he said after a moment of hesitation. "I'll take a bouquet of those blue ones."

"They're dyed blue daisies," the woman informed him as if she knew he wouldn't recognize a dandelion from a daffodil.

She rolled them into a cone of white tissue and handed them to him.

"Thanks." He told her to keep the change and started off back down the weathered-brick street.

He'd feel a whole lot better armed with a box of Godiva chocolates as well, he thought as he counted the storefronts back to her shop.

As he neared it his steps faltered. What could he possibly say to her? He clutched at the cone of flowers, his hands sweating all over the thin paper.

Swallowing the knot of fear in his throat, he peered through the wavy glass. He couldn't see Fiona, but there was an "open" sign in the window. She had to be there.

Squaring his shoulders, he tucked the bouquet behind his back and turned the brass knob. The door opened with the bright tinkle of a bell.

Fragrant smells of fine furniture polish and beeswax greeted him, teasing at his senses. Antiques of every description vied for space in the quaintly cluttered shop. He stood still in the center of it, taking in Fiona's world, breathing in the essence of it.

Each treasure she'd chosen and restored defined the woman Fiona was. Beautiful. Warm. Caring.

"I'll be right with you," she sang out in that voice that haunted his dreams.

She didn't glance up from the old, tarnished teapot she was busily polishing. It gave him a moment to observe her, and in that moment he knew he'd been right to come.

"Nick?"

Soft surprise filled her eyes when she saw him, quickly replaced by something else—alarm. Wariness shimmered in their green depths, and he knew he'd hurt her badly, though it had never been his intent.

He also knew he couldn't hurt her all over again.

"Is . . . is something wrong?" she asked. "Has something happened to Dad . . . or Winnie?"

She thought that was the reason he'd come, not that he'd had to see her. "No, everyone's fine," he quickly reassured her.

He wasn't certain, however, that these words applied to himself. Just the sight of her made him ache with the need to touch her again, fold her into his arms, and never let her go.

She let out the breath she'd been holding and he fought down the urge to go to her. She'd never looked more beautiful to him than she did at that moment. Or more fragile.

A soft, mint-green summer dress draped her feminine frame, and her long, glorious hair coiled around her face, framing it with its burnished red glow. Only the smudge of tarnish on the tip of her pretty nose kept her from looking like she'd just strolled across the lawn at a garden party.

Just then he remembered the flowers he had hidden behind his back, their stems no doubt tortured from his strangled grip on them. "I brought you something," he said, and presented them to her.

Her eyes widened and her mouth curved up in a pleased smile. She set down the silver teapot she'd been holding and wiped her palms on a soft towel. "Oh Nick, for me?"

"For you."

Their hands touched briefly as she took the bouquet from him. The inadvertent brush sent a thousand-watt bolt of electricity streaking through him, nearly rocking him off his feet.

"I'll just put them in water," she said quietly.

He swallowed against the dryness in his throat as she bent to search a glass-fronted cabinet for the proper vase. Finding one that pleased her, she turned to a small sink and filled the vase with water.

"Why are you in Boston? A case?" She tossed the question over her shoulder as she arranged the flowers.

"A case?"

Nick wanted to lie and tell her yes. He wanted to sneak away before he could hurt her more. He'd seen the faint blue tinges of fatigue beneath her eyes, suspected the same sleepless nights that haunted him had haunted her—and he hated that. Still, he knew a lie would stick in his throat.

"No, not a case. Fiona, I—I had to come."

She spun around and the green of her eyes swamped him.

"I missed you," he added, his voice a definite quaver.

Fiona wasn't sure she'd heard Nick right. She had wanted him to come; she had wanted to go to him. She'd wanted all this misery to end.

From the looks of him, Nick had been suffering too. The desert blue of his eyes had faded to the dusk of an evening sky and something had happened to that smile she remembered. She couldn't believe he was here. In her shop. In the middle of the morning.

For a moment, when she'd first seen him, she had thought she'd conjured him up out of her desperation, from the dreams that played out in her mind at night.

She didn't dare ponder why he'd come. For now, at least, it was enough that he had, that he was here. She wouldn't wonder why.

"I—I missed you, too, Nick." The words tumbled out and it was too late to snatch them back. "Even though I shouldn't. I know how you feel about *us* . . . about—"

He took the vase from her hands, setting it down on her small, disorderly work counter. She shivered as he stroked his thumb along the side of her cheek. She wanted him so much, she ached from it.

"You don't know how I feel about us, Fiona. I never told you, because I didn't want to say the words and end up hurting you in the process. I didn't want to bear the hurt myself, the disappointment, when what we shared was crushed into dust at our feet."

Fiona squeezed her eyes shut. Nothing had changed, then. Nick didn't believe love could survive in the imperfect world he saw around him.

Oh, why had he come here? Why did he want to say all this to her again? She was sure she couldn't endure it—not a second time.

"Fiona, we need to talk. Can you put a 'closed' sign in the window? Play hooky with me today?"

She swallowed hard. A part of her wanted to, another part knew she'd only be hurt all over again. But she had to share one more moment with Nick—just one. And as his eyes caressed her face she knew she couldn't summon the strength to refuse him.

"All right. I'll just set the answering machine and lock up."

Nick had never felt time creep by so slowly, but finally Fiona flipped the sign in the shop's window and they pulled the front door shut behind them with a click.

They retrieved his rental car from the hotel, and he found his way out of the city, driving along a meandering route that followed the shoreline. They stopped at a roadside place for lunch, devouring the fresh clams like two hungry urchins.

After lunch they strolled on a quiet beach,

her hand tucked into his, softly, securely. It felt so right, so perfect, so natural there—as if there were no problems, no barriers. And maybe there weren't—except for the ones they'd erected themselves. *He'd* erected. To preserve his heart.

He loved Fiona. If there'd been any doubt in his mind about that, seeing her again had answered it. He also knew he couldn't live without her.

"What did you want to talk to me about, Nick?" Her voice was soft and low against the rush of the ocean. He wanted to hear it always, a throaty purr in the morning, a husky growl at night when they made love.

He turned to her then and drew her against him. She felt so soft, so fragile. "I want you, Fiona." He whispered the words into her hair. "I need you in my life. I know that now; I know I should never have let you go."

Fiona drew back and gazed up into his eyes. Something shimmered there that she wanted to believe was love, but she didn't dare let herself hope. She had to protect her heart. Nick had stolen it; she couldn't let him crush it.

But then he lowered his mouth to hers and kissed her. A kiss hot and full of want, the same want that surged through her. She was lost in the heat of him—hopelessly lost.

Finally he broke the kiss and gazed down

at her, vulnerable and needy. "I love you," he murmured. "Do you think you could love me?"

"Oh, Nick, I already do."

He studied her face as if searching for doubt in her answer. Lord help her, she had none—in spite of the risk she knew she was taking.

"I've hurt you, Fiona. You believed in love and happily ever after and I—I couldn't . . ."

"Oh, Nick . . ." She would teach him, if only he would let her. She'd teach him if it took the rest of their lives.

He drew her down on a rock at the edge of the sea, kissed her again, then stroked her face. "There's so much I have to say to you, and I don't know how to start."

She didn't want to talk; she only wanted to taste him again, all his fire and passion, all that she had missed the past two weeks. But Nick was right—there was too much unsaid between them.

"Just start," she said, her words a bare whisper.

He stood up, then began to pace the sand in front of them. "I'd been seeing the wrong side of love in my practice, Fiona, the side that got tangled up in selfishness and mistrust—and all the other things that can turn a marriage sour."

"I know, Nick."

He went on. "The other day I had a couple reconcile. They'd changed their mind about going to court. They wanted to try to make their marriage work again."

"And that doesn't happen often in divorce cases?"

"Not often enough. But when it did, when they decided to try again, I realized I'd been focusing only on the negative instead of the beauty of the marriages that do make it. I thought of how my own marriage had crumbled and I was certain that love was a fabrication of the mind, a nonreality. I refused to look further—until I came here, Fiona. Until I looked into your eyes and saw what I would be giving up."

Fiona jumped up and went to him, flinging her arms around his neck. She kissed him long and hard and deep. "Oh, Nick . . ."

He held her close against him, as if afraid of losing her.

"I was miserable after you left, Fiona. I blamed that misery on everything but the real reason: you were gone. I tried a vacation, to get away. It lasted two days. Auntie mentioned you in every postcard—as if I needed any reminders that you weren't there, that I couldn't reach out and hold you and kiss you like this."

She smiled through the tears welling in her eyes. "I was every bit as miserable, Nick. I

Here Comes the Bride

tried to work, I tried to forget you, but I couldn't do either. I could only *miss* you."

Nick kissed her again, slowly this time, drinking her in hungrily. She tasted slightly salty from the air and the ocean.

She tasted like forever—and forever was what he wanted with her.

"Marry me, Fiona," he whispered. "Marry me soon."

"As soon as you want, Nick."

Fiona could hardly wait to start showing him that love was a permanent commodity.

And she knew just the place to start—the antique rosewood four-poster in her bedroom.

She wanted to make love with him in it all afternoon. And all through the night. She wanted to wake up with him in the morning, knowing it was the first day of forever for them.

She kissed her way to his ear, then whispered into it all the things she wanted to do to him in that big bed.

Nick broke every speed limit getting back to Fiona's shop. Making sure the "closed" sign was firmly in place, he carried her up the staircase to her apartment.

He had no trouble locating the big bed she'd mentioned and had no trouble getting her out of her clothes. But it seemed to take an interminably long time for Fiona to get him out of his—*and* to check out his sexy briefs.

Her gaze took him in, slowly, thoroughly. "Tiger stripes," she said, smiling up at him with an ever-so-naughty curve of her lips.

She proceeded to peel them off of him, her touch soft and dangerous. Then she led him to her bed.

EPILOGUE

"This is the last suitcase," Fiona said, setting it by the front door for Nick to carry down to the car for the trip to the airport.

She couldn't believe that two small babies and one husband could generate that much luggage.

"Are you sure we packed everything?" Nick asked, counting the five bags.

"If it's not in the suitcases, we don't need it. Besides, if we don't hurry, we're going to miss our flight."

Fiona was ready to escape this part of Boston's long winter and spend a few weeks in the desert. Her father and Winnie were anxious to see the twins again. It would be a family reunion. Even Camille would be there. She was coming from India and said she had wonderful news to tell everyone.

Fiona hoped that meant there would be another wedding in the gazebo soon, like the one Winnie and Walter had had, like Fiona's and Nick's a few months later.

She still smiled when she thought of her wedding day—and her wedding night. Nick could make her body sing with just his touch.

Their love had grown, deepening into something that left no doubt in her husband's mind that happily ever after did exist. She and Nick had created it for themselves.

They had also created two wonderful babies that occupied their days—and sometimes their nights when colic or bouts of teething kept them awake.

They'd long ago outgrown their small apartment over Fiona's shop, but Fiona hated to move and give up the warmth and coziness the four of them shared there.

She had help in the shop now—Peggy, her new assistant, who would run Antiques 'n Such while she and Nick were away. Nick had given up his Las Vegas practice. With his talents, he'd been quickly welcomed into one of Boston's most prestigious law firms. He handled only the occasional divorce case now, having decided to move on to other legal arenas.

"The car's packed," Nick announced. "Are you ready? Walter's probably already at the airport in Vegas, he's so anxious to see

Matt and Mark." He kissed the twins, then scooped them up, one in each arm. "I hope Walter didn't drive that old sedan of his."

Fiona smiled, then reached up and met Nick's lips. "You know Dad likes that old car. It makes him feel secure."

She laughed at Nick's pained expression but couldn't help but bask in her own wonderful feeling of security as Nick ushered his small family out the door. Her world was rich, full of enough passion and love to last a lifetime. A lifetime of loving Nick and being loved by him.

THE EDITOR'S CORNER

Escape the summer doldrums with the four new, exciting LOVESWEPT romances available next month. With our authors piloting a whirlwind tour through the jungles of human emotion, everyday experiences take a direct turn into thrill, so prepare to hang on to the edge of your seat!

With her trademark humor and touching emotion, Patt Bucheister crafts an irresistible story of mismatched dreamers surprised and transformed by unexpected love in **WILD IN THE NIGHT**, LOVESWEPT #750. She expects him to be grateful that his office is no longer an impossible mess, but instead adventurer Paul Forge tells efficiency expert Coral Bentley he wants all his junk back exactly where he had left it! When she refuses, little does she realize she is tangling with a renegade who never takes no for an answer, a man of mystery who will issue a challenge that will draw her into the seductive unknown. Hold on while Patt Bucheister skillfully navigates this ride on the unpredictable rapids of romance.

The excitement continues with **CATCH ME IF YOU CAN,** LOVESWEPT #751. In this cat-and-mouse adventure, Victoria Leigh introduces a pair of adversaries who can't resist trying to get the best of each other. Drawn to the fortress by Abigail Roberts's mysterious invitation, Tanner Flynn faces the woman who is his fiercest rival—and vows to explore the heat that still sparks between them! He had awakened her desire years before, then stunned her by refusing to claim her innocence. Join Victoria Leigh on this sexy chase filled with teasing and flirting with utter abandon.

Take one part bad-boy hero, add a feisty redhead, raise the temperature to flame-hot and what you get is a **PAGAN'S PARADISE,** LOVESWEPT #752, from Susan Connell. Jack Stratford is hold-your-breath-handsome, a blue-eyed rogue who knows everyone in San Rafael, but photographer Joanna McCall refuses to believe his warning that she is in danger—except perhaps from his stolen kisses! She isn't looking for a broken heart, just a little adventure . . . until Jack ignites a fire in her blood only he can satisfy. Take a walk on the wild side with Susan Connell as your guide.

In **UP CLOSE AND PERSONAL,** LOVESWEPT #753, Diane Pershing weaves a moving tale of survivors who find sweet sanctuary in each other's arms. A master at getting others to reveal their secrets, Evan Stone never lets a woman get close enough to touch the scars that brand his soul. But when small-town mom Chris McConnell dares to confess the sorrows that haunt her, her courage awakens a yearning long-denied in his own heart. A poignant journey of rough and tender love from talented Diane Pershing.

Happy reading!

With warmest wishes,

Beth de Guzman

Shauna Summers

Beth de Guzman
Senior Editor

Shauna Summers
Associate Editor

P.S. Watch for these spectacular Bantam women's fiction titles slated for August: In **BEFORE I WAKE**, Loveswept star Terry Lawrence weaves the beloved fairy tale *Sleeping Beauty* into a story so enthralling it will keep you up long into the night; highly acclaimed author Susan Krinard ventures into outerspace with **STARCROSSED**, a story of a beautiful aristocrat who risks a forbidden love with a dangerously seductive man born of an alien race; *USA Today* bestselling author Patricia Potter follows the success of WANTED and RELENTLESS with **DEFIANT**, another spectacular love story, this time of a dangerous man who discovers the redeeming power of love. See next month's LOVESWEPTs for a preview of these compelling novels. And immediately following this page, look for a preview of the wonderful romances from Bantam that *are available now*!

Don't miss these extraordinary books
by your favorite Bantam authors

On sale in June:

MYSTIQUE
by Amanda Quick

VIOLET
by Jane Feather

MOTHER LOVE
by Judith Henry Wall

HEAVEN SENT
by Pamela Morsi

THE WARLORD
by Elizabeth Elliott

> "One of the hottest and most prolific writers in romance today."
> —*USA Today*

MYSTIQUE

by the *New York Times* bestselling author
AMANDA QUICK
available in hardcover

Who better to tell you about this dazzling romance than the author herself? Here, then, is a personal letter from Amanda Quick:

Dear Reader:

Any man who is dangerous enough to become a living legend is probably best avoided by a sensible, intelligent lady who has determined to live a quiet, cloistered life. But sometimes a woman has to work with what's available. And as it happens, the man they call Hugh the Relentless is available . . . for a price.

Lady Alice, the heroine of my next book, *Mystique*, does not hesitate to do what must be done. She requires the services of a strong knight to help her escape her uncle's clutches; Hugh, on the other hand, requires assistance in the hunt for a missing gemstone

—and a woman willing to masquerade as his betrothed.

Alice decides that she and this dark legend of a man can do business together. She strikes a bold bargain with him. But you know what they say about the risks of bargaining with the devil . . .

Mystique is the fast-paced tale of a man and a woman who form an alliance, one that puts them on a collision course with passion, danger—and each other. It is the story of a ruthless man who is bent on vengeance and a lady who has her heart set on a studious, contemplative life—a life that definitely does not include a husband.

These two were made for each other.

I hope you will enjoy *Mystique*. When it comes to romance, there is something very special about the medieval setting, don't you think? It was a time that saw the first full flowering of some of the best-loved and most romantic legends, tales that we still enjoy in many forms today. Hugh and Alice are part of that larger-than-life period in history but their story is timeless. When it comes to affairs of the human heart, the era does not really matter. But then, as a reader of romance, you already know that.

Until the next book.

Love,

Amanda Quick

"An author to treasure."
—*Romantic Times*

VIOLET
by bestselling author
JANE FEATHER

Sure to continue her spectacular rise to stardom, VIOLET is vintage Jane Feather—passionate, adventurous, and completely enjoyable from the opening paragraph.

"Take off the rest of your clothes."

"What! All of them? In front of you?" She looked outraged, and yet somehow he wasn't convinced by this display of maidenly modesty.

"Yes, all of them," he affirmed evenly. "I doubt even you will take off from the far bank stark naked."

Tamsyn turned away from him and unfastened her skirt. Damn the man for being such a perspicacious bastard.

She dropped the shirt to the ground, loosened the string at the waist of her drawers, and kicked them off.

"Satisfied, Colonel?"

For a moment he ignored the double-edged question that threw a contemptuous challenge. His eyes ran down the lean, taut body that seemed to thrum with energy. He realized that the illusion of fragility came from her diminutive stature; unclothed, she had the compact, smooth-muscled body of an athlete, limber and arrow straight. His gaze lingered on the small, pointed breasts, the slight flare of her hips, the tangle of pale hair at the base of her belly.

It was the most desirable little body. His breath quickened, and his nostrils flared as he fought down the torrent of arousal.

"Perfectly," he drawled. "I find myself perfectly satisfied."

Julian watched as she stood poised above the water. The back view was every bit as arousing as the front, he reflected dreamily. Then she rose on her toes, raised her arms, and dove cleanly into the swift-running river.

He walked to the edge of the bank, waiting for the bright fair head to surface. But there was no sign of La Violette. It was as if she'd dove and disappeared.

He was pulling off his boots, tearing at the buttons of his tunic without conscious decision. He flung his sword belt to the grass, yanked off his britches and his shirt, and dove into the river as close as possible to where he believed his prisoner had gone in.

Tamsyn surfaced on the far side of the rocks as soon as she heard the splash as he entered the water.

She leaped onto the bank, hidden by the rocks from the swimmer on the other side, and shook the water from her body with the vigor of a small dog.

Julian came up for air, numbed with cold, knowing that he shouldn't stay in the water another minute, yet forcing himself to go down for one more look. As he prepared to dive, he glanced toward the bank and saw a pale shadow against the rock, and then it was gone.

His bellow of fury roared through the peaceful early morning on the banks of the Guadiana.

Tamsyn swore to herself and picked up her heels, racing across the flat mossy ground toward the small brush-covered hill.

Julian, however, had been a sprinter in his school days, and his long legs ate up the distance between them.

She fell to her knees with a cry of annoyance that changed to a shriek of alarmed fury as Julian hurled himself forward and his fingers closed over her ankle. She hadn't realized he was that close.

"*Espadachín!*" she threw at him. "I may be a bandit, but you're a brute and a bully, Colonel. Let me up."

"No."

The simple negative stunned her. She stared up into his face that was now as calm and equable as if they were sitting in some drawing room.

Her astonished silence lasted barely a second; then she launched a verbal assault of such richness and variety that the colonel's jaw dropped. She moved seamlessly within three languages, and the insults and oaths would have done an infantryman proud.

"Cease your ranting, girl!" He recovered from his surprise and did the only thing he could think of, bringing his mouth to hers to silence the stream of invective. His grip on her wrists tightened with his fingers on her chin, and his body was heavy on hers as he leaned over her supine figure.

Then everything became confused. There was rage—wild rage—but it was mixed with a different passion, every bit as savage . . .

MOTHER LOVE
by Judith Henry Wall

"Wall keeps you turning the pages."
—*San Francisco Chronicle*

There is no love as strong or as enduring as the love of a mother for her child. But what if that child commits an act that goes against a woman's deepest beliefs? Is there a limit to a mother's love?

Karen Billingsly's perfect life shatters one night with her son's unexpected return from college. Though neither Chad nor his attorney father will tell Karen what's wrong, she begins to suspect her son has done something unthinkable. And Karen, the perfect wife and mother, must decide just how far a mother will go to protect her son.

Out of habit, Karen ignored the first two rings of the telephone. Phone calls in the night were for Roger—frantic parents of felonious teenagers, wives fearful of estranged husbands, the accused calling from jail, even the dying wanting to execute deathbed wills.

Karen rolled over to his side of the bed and picked up the phone.

It was Chad. She looked at the clock. Not yet five. And instantly, she was sitting up. Awake. Worried.

"Where's Dad?" he asked.

"Padre Island."

"Oh, yeah—the fishing trip. I forgot. That's why you guys aren't coming down tomorrow for the game. When's he coming back?"

"His plane ticket says Sunday morning, but Tropical Storm Clifton is heading their way—and threatening to turn itself into a hurricane. Your father's trying to leave tomorrow instead, but so are lots of other people."

"But you are expecting him tomorrow?" Chad asked.

"I hope so. Are you all right?" Karen half expected him to say he was calling from a police station. Another DUI. Or worse.

"Yeah. Sure. I just wanted you to know I'm on my way home. I didn't want you to think you had a burglar when I come in."

"You're coming home *now*?" Karen asked. "It's awfully early."

He laughed. A thin, tired laugh. "Or awfully late, depending how you look at it. The house had a big party, and I haven't been to bed yet. I need to spend the weekend studying, and with a home football game, this place will be crawling with alums and parents in just a few hours. We're already overflowing with Kansas State guys down for the game. I'll get more done at home."

"Sounds like a good idea. You might even get a home-cooked meal or two."

"That'd be great. Love you, Mom. A lot."

"You sure you're okay?"

"Fine. Go back to sleep."

Karen hung up the phone, curled her body back into its sleep position and closed her eyes. But her mind kept replaying the conversation. Maybe it was from too much beer or the late hour, but Chad's voice had sounded strained—with just a trace of a quiver, like when he used to come padding in the bedroom during a thunderstorm, back when she had been Mommie instead of Mom. "I can't sleep," he would say as he crawled in beside her. And she would curl her body protectively around his and feel him immediately go limp with sleep. She missed that part of motherhood. The physical part. A small, sturdy body pressed next to her own. Plump little arms around her neck. A tender young neck to kiss. She didn't get to touch either of her children enough. With Melissa, it was a pat every now and then, an occasional hug. Chad, after years of adolescent avoidance of his mother's every kiss and touch, now actually reached for her sometimes, but mostly on arrival and departure, not often enough.

She rolled onto her back, then tried her stomach. Her son had sounded worried.

When finally she heard him come in, she went downstairs.

He was standing inside the back door, looking around the kitchen, a backpack and small duffel both hung over one shoulder. He looked almost puzzled, like there was something different about the room. Karen took a quick look around. But it was the same cheerful room it had always been—big round table, captain's chairs, a large braided rug on the brick floor. She slipped her arms around her son who was no longer a boy. He was bigger than his father, more solid. Yet, it was hard to think of him as a man, hard to call him a man.

"Did you and Brenda have a fight?" she asked.

"No," he said, hugging her back, clinging a bit, putting his cheek against her hair. "She's in Tulsa visiting her sister. I'm just feeling shitty from too much beer. Maybe I should have done without the whole fraternity bit—the partying gets out of hand. And some of the brothers are low-life jerks."

"And some of them are nice guys. I can't believe

you're missing a home game," Karen said, relinquishing her hold on him.

"It's only Kansas State. I would have hung around if you and Dad were coming down. But I need to study. And sleep."

"Well, save some time for your sister. She could use a big brother every now and then."

Karen insisted that he take a couple of aspirin with a glass of milk to waylay a hangover. He looked as though the light was already hurting his eyes.

"You want something to eat?"

"No. We had pizza at the party. Two dozen of them."

He followed her up the stairs. She hugged him again outside the door to his room. "It's good to have you home, son. I miss having you around."

"Yeah. I miss you guys, too. Sometimes I wonder why I was in such a hurry to grow up and leave home. I don't have a mom around now to bandage skinned knees and proofread papers."

Karen went back to her bedroom and opened the drapes. The sprawling backyard looked black and white in the hazy first light. Surrealistic even. Like a dreamscape.

She went to the bathroom, then returned to her bed, and sat on the side by the window, staring out at the predawn sky. The weatherman had promised another warm day. Indian summer. Daytime temperatures once again in the upper 80s. Another balmy evening—like last night. Much too warm for a fire in the big stone fireplace in the fraternity house living room.

But her son's clothes had smelled of smoke.

THE WARLORD
by Elizabeth Elliott

"Elizabeth Elliott is an exciting find for romance readers everywhere."
—*New York Times* bestselling author
Amanda Quick

Scarred by war and the dark secret of his birth, Kenric of Montague had no wish for a wife . . . until he beheld the magnificent woman pledged to be his bride. Yet even as Kenric gave in to his aching hunger to possess her, he vowed she would never tame his savage heart. But then a treacherous plot threatens Kenric and his new wife, and now he must fight his most dangerous battle yet for their lives and for his soul.

"Would now be a poor time to ask a question?" Tess raised her eyebrows hopefully, but the baron's forbidding expression didn't change. Nor did he answer. Rudeness seemed to be his most dominant trait. Unable to meet his intimidating gaze a moment longer, she casually turned her attention to the road, ignoring his silence. "I was wondering what name I should call you by."

"I am your lord and master, Lady," he finally answered, his tone condescending. "You may address me as Milord, or Baron, or . . . Husband."

The man's arrogance left Tess speechless. She considered thanking him—most sarcastically—for allowing her to speak at all, but thought better of the idea. She would behave civilly for the duration of this farce, even if he did not.

"What I meant to ask was your given name, *Husband*. I know your titles, Baron Montague, but I do not know your Christian name."

The man had the audacity to smile at her. Tess quickly dropped her gaze back to the road, half afraid she would betray her anger and smile back. The man was much too appealing by half. That is, when he wasn't being openly rude. Thank goodness he liked to frown. She wasn't at all sure she liked the strange emotions that seemed to befuddle her senses when he didn't look ready to murder her.

"My name is Kenric."

Though her hood was between them, Tess could almost feel his lips against her ear and his breath against her cheek. She marveled at the way his deep voice vibrated right through her body and wondered why the words seemed to steal her breath away.

"You may call me by such whenever we are alone, *Wife*." Kenric expected to get some sort of reaction when he stressed the word 'wife,' but Tess didn't say a word. He pulled her hood aside, surprised to see her smiling.

"You find some humor in my name?" he asked. Her smile grew broader. "Well?"

"Hm?" she inquired absently.

"Why are you smiling?" Kenric demanded, his expression softening when she raised her head and looked up at him. The sweet, faraway look in her eyes was enchanting.

"Your voice," Tess answered dreamily. "I can feel it. Right here." She placed her palm between her breasts, a soft laugh in her voice. "It tickles."

HEAVEN SENT
by Pamela Morsi

"Morsi's stories are filled with lively narration and generous doses of humor."
—*Publisher's Weekly*

When virtuous Hannah Bunch set out to trap herself a husband, she hardly dreamed she'd be compromised by a smoldering, blue-eyed stranger. Her reputation shattered, she promises to honor and cherish him always—never suspecting that his first touch will spark an unquenchable flame and his secret will threaten her life.

"Violet! Bring me my gun!"

Inside the wellhouse, Hannah Bunch woke from her warm, pleasant dream, startled to hear the sound of her father's angry voice. Disoriented at first, she quickly realized that everything was going as expected. This was a crucial part of her plan, a difficult part, but one that was essential. Her father would be understandably angry, she had known that from the beginning. But it was her father who had taught her that nothing worth having was achieved without sacrifice. A few embarrassing moments could hardly be counted against a lifetime of contentment.

She knew that more than one couple from the community had anticipated their wedding night, and rather than condemning them her father had always been understanding and forgiving. She had counted on that spirit of forgiveness, but there was no mercy in him right now. He was furious and he seemed to Hannah to be talking crazily, directing his anger to the man who stood silently behind her.

"People told me not to trust you, that you're a heathen with no morals, a son of a drunken squawman. But I said a man must be judged on his own merits! The more fool me! I invite you into my home, feed you at my table, and this is how you repay me, by ruining my daughter!"

"Papa, please don't be angry," she pleaded, leaving the door of the wellhouse and walking toward her father with her arms outstretched, entreating him. "I love him, Papa, and I think that he loves me," she lied.

Her father's look, if possible, became even more murderous. Her brother, Leroy snorted an obscenity in protest. She grabbed her father's clenched fists and brought them up to her face in supplication. "He's a good man, Papa. You know that as well as I."

The crowd of people stood watching in shock as Violet, who had heard the commotion and her husband's call for a weapon, came running with his old squirrel gun, as though she'd thought some rabid animal had got shut up in the wellhouse. Seeing her stepdaughter, clad only in her thin cotton nightgown, she stood stunned in disbelief, but retained the good sense not to give her husband the weapon.

"Papa, we want to be married," Hannah pleaded, praying silently that Will would not dispute her statement. "Please, we want your blessing."

Her brothers exchanged looks of furious disbelief and righteous indignation.

"You're a dead man!" Rafe, the youngest, threatened.

Hannah was tempted to go over and box his ears.

"Give me that gun!" Ned ordered Violet, but she gripped it tighter.

Hannah's patience with the whole group was wearing thin. It wasn't as if she were a green girl, she was a grown woman of twenty-six and was thoroughly entitled to make her own mistakes.

"I love him, don't you understand?" she lied. "I want to be with him."

"That low-down snake doesn't deserve the likes of you, Miss Hannah!" a voice just to the right of her father shouted in anger. "What's got into you messing with a decent farmer's daughter?" he yelled at the man behind her.

The voice captured Hannah's immediate attention. She turned toward it, shocked. Will Sample, the man she planned to marry, was standing in a group of men staring angrily at the wellhouse.

With a feeling of unreality, Hannah turned toward the object of their anger. In the doorway of the small building, with his hands upraised like a captured bank robber was Henry Lee Watson, a man Hannah barely knew.

And don't miss these electrifying romances from Bantam Books, on sale in July:

DEFIANT
by Pat Potter

"A shining talent."
—*Affaire de Coeur*

STARCROSSED
by Susan Krinard

"Susan Krinard has set the standard for today's fantasy romance."
—*Affaire de Coeur*

BEFORE I WAKE
by Terry Lawrence

"Terry Lawrence makes the sparks really fly."
—*Romantic Times*

OFFICIAL RULES NO PURCHASE NECESSARY

To enter the sweepstakes outlined below, you must respond by the date specified and follow all entry instructions published elsewhere in this offer.

DREAM COME TRUE SWEEPSTAKES

Sweepstakes begins 9/1/94, ends 1/15/96. To qualify for the Early Bird Prize, entry must be received by the date specified elsewhere in this offer. Winners will be selected in random drawings on 2/29/96 by an independent judging organization whose decisions are final. Early Bird winner will be selected in a separate drawing from among all qualifying entries.

Odds of winning determined by total number of entries received. Distribution not to exceed 300 million.

Estimated maximum retail value of prizes: Grand (1) $25,000 (cash alternative $20,000); First (1) $2,000; Second (1) $750; Third (50) $75; Fourth (1,000) $50; Early Bird (1) $5,000. Total prize value: $86,500.

Automobile and travel trailer must be picked up at a local dealer; all other merchandise prizes will be shipped to winners. Awarding of any prize to a minor will require written permission of parent/guardian. If a trip prize is won by a minor, s/he must be accompanied by parent/legal guardian. Trip prizes subject to availability and must be completed within 12 months of date awarded. Blackout dates may apply. Early Bird trip is on a space available basis and does not include port charges, gratuities, optional shore excursions and onboard personal purchases. Prizes are not transferable or redeemable for cash except as specified. No substitution for prizes except as necessary due to unavailability. Travel trailer and/or automobile license and registration fees are winners' responsibility as are any other incidental expenses not specified herein.

Early Bird Prize may not be offered in some presentations of this sweepstakes. Grand through third prize winners will have the option of selecting any prize offered at level won. All prizes will be awarded. Drawing will be held at 204 Center Square Road, Bridgeport, NJ 08014. Winners need not be present. For winners list (available in June, 1996), send a self-addressed, stamped envelope by 1/15/96 to: Dream Come True Winners, P.O. Box 572, Gibbstown, NJ 08027.

THE FOLLOWING APPLIES TO THE SWEEPSTAKES ABOVE:

No purchase necessary. No photocopied or mechanically reproduced entries will be accepted. Not responsible for lost, late, misdirected, damaged, incomplete, illegible, or postage-die mail. Entries become the property of sponsors and will not be returned.

Winner(s) will be notified by mail. Winner(s) may be required to sign and return an affidavit of eligibility/release within 14 days of date on notification or an alternate may be selected. Except where prohibited by law, entry constitutes permission to use of winners' names, hometowns, and likenesses for publicity without additional compensation. Void where prohibited or restricted. All federal, state, provincial, and local laws and regulations apply.

All prize values are in U.S. currency. Presentation of prizes may vary; values at a given prize level will be approximately the same. All taxes are winners' responsibility.

Canadian residents, in order to win, must first correctly answer a time-limited skill testing question administered by mail. Any litigation regarding the conduct and awarding of a prize in this publicity contest by a resident of the province of Quebec may be submitted to the Regie des loteries et courses du Quebec.

Sweepstakes is open to legal residents of the U.S., Canada, and Europe (in those areas where made available) who have received this offer.

Sweepstakes in sponsored by Ventura Associates, 1211 Avenue of the Americas, New York, NY 10036 and presented by independent businesses. Employees of these, their advertising agencies and promotional companies involved in this promotion, and their immediate families, agents, successors, and assignees shall be ineligible to participate in the promotion and shall not be eligible for any prizes covered herein. SWP 3/95

DON'T MISS THESE FABULOUS BANTAM WOMEN'S FICTION TITLES

On sale in June

From the blockbuster author of nine consecutive *New York Times* bestsellers comes a tantalizing tale of a quest for a dazzling crystal.

MYSTIQUE by Amanda Quick

"One of the hottest and most prolific writers in romance today."—USA Today
Available in hardcover   ____ 09698-2 $21.95/$24.95 in Canada

VIOLET by Jane Feather

"An author to treasure."—Romantic Times

From the extraordinary pen of Jane Feather, nationally bestselling author of *Valentine*, comes a bewitching tale of a beautiful bandit who's waging a dangerous game of vengeance—and betting everything on love.   ____ 56471-4 $5.50/$6.99

MOTHER LOVE by Judith Henry Wall

"Wall keeps you turning the pages."—San Francisco Chronicle

There is no love as strong or enduring as the love of a mother for her child. But what if that child commits an act that goes against a woman's deepest beliefs? Is there a limit to a mother's love? Judith Henry Wall, whose moving stories and finely drawn characters have earned her critical praise and a devoted readership, has written her most compelling novel yet.   ____ 56789-6 $5.99/$7.50

THE WARLORD by Elizabeth Elliott

"Elizabeth Elliott is an exciting find for romance readers everywhere.... Spirited, sensual, tempestuous romance at its best."
—New York Times *bestselling author Amanda Quick*

In the bestselling tradition of Teresa Medeiros and Elizabeth Lowell, *The Warlord* is a magical and captivating tale of a woman who must dare to love the man she fears the most.   ____ 56910-4 $5.50/$6.99

Ask for these books at your local bookstore or use this page to order.

Please send me the books I have checked above. I am enclosing $____ (add $2.50 to cover postage and handling). Send check or money order, no cash or C.O.D.'s, please.

Name _____

Address _____

City/State/Zip _____

Send order to: Bantam Books, Dept. FN158, 2451 S. Wolf Rd., Des Plaines, IL 60018
Allow four to six weeks for delivery.
Prices and availability subject to change without notice.   FN 158 7/95